A Daring Dilemma

A Daring Dilemma

Nina Coombs Pykare

Five Star • Waterville, Maine

Five Star Romance Series.

Published in 2001 in conjunction with
Maureen Moran Agency.

Set in 11 pt. Plantin by Al Chase.

Printed in the United States on permanent paper.

Library of Congress Cataloging-in-Publication Data

Pykare, Nina.
    A daring dilemma / Nina Coombs Pykare.
      p. cm.
    ISBN 0-7862-3501-2 (hc : alk. paper)
    I. Title.
    PS3566.Y48 D28 2001
    813'.54—dc21   2001033733

For David II

1

"My dearest Hortense, there is no doubt about it! Ravenworth is the man!"

Licia Dudley, peering over the rim of a delicate Wedgwood cup at her vehement Mama, suppressed a shudder. Mama had always been a little difficult, and Papa's death had only made her more so. She'd always been given to flights of fancy. But this latest start of hers . . .

"Dorothea, pray have some sense!" Aunt Hortense's stately face and majestic mien were the opposite of Mama's butterfly smallness and quickness. And Aunt Hortense had a tongue that could be quite biting. Not that Mama ever took any notice of it. Mama was like that proverbial runaway horse: Once she took the bit between her teeth, there was no stopping her.

Still, Aunt Hortense was making a valiant attempt. "I'll grant you the chit has a look about her," she continued with a frosty smile to Desiree. "But she's not the sort for Ravenworth. It just won't suit. Why, the man will eat her alive."

From a delicate Hepplewhite chair Desiree turned to her sister. Her blue eyes widened in fear. "Licia, I don't want—"

"Hush, my dear." Licia automatically patted her sister's hand. "It will be all right. I promise."

In truth, Dezzie *should* have a husband. She needed someone to look after her, someone with more sense than Mama. Oh, Mama was entirely right about one thing—there was no one back home in York who was suitable. But this trip to London . . .

Mama took up her needlepoint, a half-finished fire screen that was supposed to show a Gothic ruin. Since Mama never picked out a misplaced stitch, and since she misplaced a great many, her endeavors in this area were almost always unrecognizable. That had never deterred her, of course.

Licia sighed again. If only she'd been able to keep Mama at home. She longed for the peaceful York countryside, for the sane and comfortable life they had led there.

Mama stitched serenely for several minutes, but since she never gave up easily, Licia was not at all surprised to hear her observe, "You said yourself that the duke should have a wife."

Aunt Hortense frowned. Dezzie pulled in a sharp breath and glanced anxiously at her sister.

"Of course the man ought to have a wife." Aunt Hortense was obviously trying for patience—and just as obviously not achieving it. "His poor mama has been saying that for many a year. But he's found no one to his liking."

"Then he's sure to like Dezzie," said Mama complacently, with one of those weird turns of perverted logic that no other mind could hope to follow.

Aunt Hortense uttered an outraged and very unladylike snort and turned to her niece. "Licia, can you not talk some sense into your mama?"

Since Licia had been attempting that very thing for many years, and with a singular lack of success, she could only shake her head. She did manage, however, to summon a smile. "Might I suggest, Aunt, that the whole question is rather speculative? I mean, surely his choice of a bride is up to the duke."

Aunt Hortense brightened considerably at this piece of common sense, and Dezzie sighed with relief.

But Mama raised her head. She was clearly not about to

give up her sentiments on such an important matter. Then, just as she opened her mouth to continue, Herberts appeared. "Callers, Your Ladyship. The Dowager Duchess of Ravenworth and the Duke."

Dezzie tugged at her sister's sleeve. "Licia—"

"Sssh," Licia whispered. "Everything will be fine." Dezzie was undeniably a pretty girl, but she was so scatterbrained. How could Mama expect her to attract a man of high station?

"Hortense, my dear," the dowager duchess said.

"Eglantine. Do sit down. And you, Your Grace."

The small, elegantly dressed woman crossed the room. She was dark and still lovely. The smile she gave her friend held warmth and affection. Licia decided she liked her.

But the duke . . . he was tall, on the dark side for an Englishman, with eyes that were almost black. He was dressed with impeccable taste in inexpressibles and coat that fit like second skin and boots that came near to blinding with their brilliance. He was quite too high-and-mighty for the likes of her, Licia thought. And he most certainly was not the man for Dezzie.

Mama put down her needlepoint and bestowed upon the visitors her most gracious smile. "I'm so pleased to meet you," she said, bubbling. "I'm Dorothea Dudley, Hortense's sister. And these are my daughters—Licia and Desiree. We've come all the way from York. Finally, after that dreadful winter. To give my darling Dezzie her come-out. My dear sister—"

The dear sister finally gathered her wits enough to interrupt this fountain of words. "Eglantine, my friend. How nice to see you."

"We've but recently returned to town ourselves," said the duchess with a nod to Mama. "David"—she cast an affectionate glance at her son—"has espoused some new farming methods. He is forever wanting to stay in the country to see that they are properly undertaken."

Licia sent the duke another glance. Perhaps she had misjudged him. Perhaps under the dandified clothes there was a man one could respect. She imagined the duke in the country, astride a restive stallion. It was a pretty picture. But it made her long for home.

"So you're going to launch another young woman," the duchess continued. "Is dear Penelope—"

Aunt Hortense frowned. "Penelope is still at home. She's out on errands at the moment. I hold that it's better to have no husband than an unsuitable one."

Mama looked about to comment on this, but fortunately the duke spoke first. "Quite right," he said. "All this marrying off results in much unneedful misery."

The duchess chuckled. "David is against the institution."

Mama gasped and gave the duke a telling glance. Fortunately, since he was looking at his mama, it escaped his notice. The duchess saw it, though. She laughed lightly. "Or so he claims. I hold that he has just not met the right young woman."

"Quite so," observed Mama. "Now take my Licia."

Oh, if only someone would, that unfortunate daughter thought. Take her far away from the effect of Mama's words.

But no such fortunate event occurred, and Mama went right on. "She's such a sensible girl. She'd make some man a very good wife. But somehow the right man has never come along."

"Perhaps he still will," observed the duke with a look of kindly condescension.

Licia stiffened and swallowed a sharp reply. She didn't need anyone's pity, least of all that of a rakish duke!

"Yes, of course," Mama rattled on. "But we are here for

Dezzie's come-out. I know *she* will find a husband. Don't you think so, Your Grace?" And Mama turned the full force of her smile on the duke.

To Licia's relief he appeared singularly unmoved by it. "Miss Desiree is a lovely young woman," he remarked dryly. "Any young man in need of a wife must agree to that."

Mama positively glowed at this and sent her sister an I-told-you-so look.

"Hasn't this been a most dreadful winter?" Aunt Hortense observed in an obvious attempt to change the subject.

"Yes, indeed," her bosom bow agreed, with a little twinkle in her eye.

The duke chuckled. "Now, Mama, didn't you tell me the Frost Fair was the most fun you'd had in ages?"

The duchess dimpled. "You dreadful boy. You weren't supposed to mention that."

The duke's eyes left his mama's and somehow encountered Licia's. She smiled before she quite realized it, and then, aware of her indiscretion, looked away. She didn't want him to think the whole family was as dotty as Mama.

"Eglantine," said Mama. "What a lovely name."

The duchess wrinkled a pert nose. "A family name. You know how those are."

"Oh, yes," said Mama. "My dear Mr. Dudley wanted me to name the girls after his mother and mine. But I had quite different ideas."

The duchess did not look even mildly interested, and the duke said "Indeed" in a tone that could mean anything.

But Mama, as always, took any reply as a sign of great interest. Though Licia cast her a quelling look, it was to no avail. Mama's eyes already had glazed over with that look that meant she was going to do it.

"Licia's real name is Delicia," Mama said. "But for some

reason she doesn't like it. Won't answer to it, in sober fact."

Feeling the duke's eyes upon her, Licia looked up. His smile was kindly but she hurried her glance away. She didn't need pity, she needed someone to silence Mama.

But no one did. "You see," Mama continued, "Licia is a special child. She comes from Dr. Graham's celebrated Celestial Bed."

Aunt Hortense's complexion, which already tended to the rosy, took on an even more crimson hue. "Really, Dorothea. This is hardly a fit subject for—"

Mama shook her head. "I'm sure it's all perfectly proper. The girls have heard the tale many times."

The dowager duchess smiled. "If you please, Hortense, I really should like to hear more. I remember hearing tales of the celebrated bed, but unfortunately I never got to visit it. Dear Dorothea, do go on."

And of course Mama did. "It was the most magnificent bed. On the dome were figures of Cupid and Psyche. And behind them stood Hymen. He's the god of weddings, you know. In one hand he held a flaming torch, of that new electricity, and the other hand supported a celestial crown, sparkling over two live turtledoves in their own little bed of roses."

Licia could not help herself. Much as she wanted to pretend he was not there, she had to see how the duke was responding to this recital. He was sitting perfectly erect, his expression attentive to the extreme. Surprisingly she could detect no indication of amusement on his face.

Most men, when Mama launched into this story, were given to sniggering behind their hands, but the duke was the perfect pattern card of politeness. Except—there it was: a little muscle that persisted in twitching at the right corner of his mouth.

She knew it. He would think the whole family had bats in the attic. Look at Mama, ranting on about a twelve-foot bed and magnetic fields. And Dezzie, who had so far not uttered a single word and looked as though she actually feared being eaten.

"Really, Dorothea," Aunt Hortense began, trying to stem Mama's prodigious flood of memory.

But Mama gave her no heed and, like a flood, swept everything before her. "The mattress was filled with sweet new wheat straw. And balm, rose leaves, lavender flowers. And spices from the Orient. Never have I smelled anything so glorious."

She paused and smiled beatifically. "And the sheets were silk. All the colors of the rainbow."

Licia felt the rosier hues rising to her own cheeks. What he must think of her, the product of such an outrageous parent!

For the hundredth time she wondered if she ought to have accepted one of the proposals that had come her way after Papa's death. But there had always been something to attend to at home. She'd feared leaving Mama to run amuck with the accounts. And anyway, there had been no one with whom matrimony had seemed at all attractive. So the years had passed and here she was, approaching the wrong side of thirty, still on the shelf. And at the moment wishing that shelf were far away in York.

"I wanted Mr. Dudley to take me back there," Mama concluded. "But that dear Dr. Graham sold up. And his mud baths were not nearly so efficacious."

"Not nearly," repeated the duke in a tone of such commiseration that Licia devoutly wished she might sink through the floor.

However, no such relief was forthcoming. The floor remained solid, and the duke remained attentive to Mama's every word.

"Ah, yes, mud baths." The duchess smiled sweetly. "If I remember rightly, they were intended for the general health."

Mama nodded. "Yes, but they were so—"

"Muddy," supplied the duke in a carefully polite tone that made Licia work hard to swallow a sudden and surprising tendency to giggle.

Not hearing the humor, Mama cast him an appreciative smile. But the duchess evidently knew her son better. She sent him a look that spoke volumes before saying to Mama, "That's quite an interesting tale." Her smile changed to a slight frown. "But I believe Hortense is right in this. It's not a thing to be discussed in the ton."

For a second Mama looked mutinous. The story of the bed was her stock-in-trade. Licia held her breath. The situation was rapidly losing whatever humor she had managed to see in it. What horrendous thing would Mama think to say next? But Mama merely directed a smile to the duke. "And you, Your Grace? What do you say?"

The duke smiled, too, all politeness. "With due respect to Miss Dudley and the fascinating details of her . . . ah, introduction to life, I find I must agree with Mama."

Did his voice hold the hint of a chuckle? But his appearance was sober, even stern.

"Such intimate details," he continued, "enlightening as they are, if bandied about, might make Miss Dudley the target of gossip. Certainly the gossipmongers have enough fuel without our endeavoring to provide them with more."

Aunt Hortense cleared her throat, but a glance from the duke kept her silenced. "And," he went on, "since you are here to find Miss Desiree a husband, it's hardly the thing to frighten the prospects off by talk that even borders on the un-seemly."

Mama looked about to argue, but then she apparently re-membered that the duke was the first man on that very list of prospects, the man she'd singled out for Dezzie. She dimpled and said, "Thank you, Your Grace, for your advice. It's most kind of you."

Kind! Oh, yes, he was kind. He wasn't laughing at them. At least not out loud. He wasn't giving Mama the set-down she clearly deserved. But *what* was the man thinking? It couldn't be anything good.

Though the conversation continued, it was most thank-fully about the latest London *on dits*. Licia, letting it all flow past her ears, endeavored to calm her ravaged nerves.

The damage was done, she told herself. The duke had heard the whole of the infamous tale. And actually, morti-fying as the experience had been for her, the duke had be-haved far better than most gentlemen.

She stole a glance at him. After the conclusion of Mama's tale he had allowed himself a more relaxed posture. His long legs were stretched out in front of him, and staring into space, he was absently making and remaking a steeple with his fin-gers.

He was obviously suffering from ennui. And no wonder, this London gossip was dreadfully dull. And so she did as she would have done at home: she moved to relieve his boredom.

"Tell me, Your Grace. What species of land improvement do you hold with?"

His head came erect and his black eyes surveyed her in-tently. "Part of it has to do with the rotating of crops. I want to—But the details will no doubt bore you."

"Oh, no." Licia shook her head. He was going to know

that at least one member of this family had some under-standing. "Not at all," she replied. "Papa was much inter-ested in land reform. He spoke to me about it often."

The duke's expression betrayed disbelief, so she con-tinued. "It's quite true. Since Papa had no sons, he used often to speak to me of his beliefs and desires. And land reform was one of them."

The duke's eyes seemed to grow lighter. "I see. Then you will be interested in knowing that . . ."

It was some time later when the dowager duchess rose to go. Her son got to his feet and bowed to Licia. "Thank you for a most stimulating conversation, Miss Dudley."

"You're welcome, I'm sure, Your Grace. I, too, enjoyed it." Conscious of Mama's eyes on her, she added, "The duke was telling us about his plans for land reform. Dezzie was most interested. Weren't you, dear?"

Dezzie's dutiful "Oh yes" would not have fooled anyone else. But Mama only saw what she wished to see—and she wished to see the duke and Dezzie getting along famously.

"Thank you, Your Grace. Dezzie's such an intelligent girl."

His grace bowed in acknowledgment, though, since Dezzie had not uttered even one word during the entire con-versation, he could hardly have formed much of an opinion of her intelligence.

"If you would accompany me to the door," said his grace in a tone meant only for Licia's ears.

She got to her feet with alacrity. And while Aunt Hortense and the duchess made their good-byes, the duke said softly to Licia, "I assure you, the tale of your—ah, of the bed will go no further. Mama and I know how to keep our tongues between our teeth."

Licia smiled. "You're most kind, Your Grace. But that's

16

Mama's favorite story. I don't know if even your words of wisdom will deter her."

"They should," he replied slowly. "Not only does such a story work against Miss Desiree's prospects, it does nothing to help yours."

For a long moment she stood, suffused in rosy warmth. This man actually thought she had prospects! But then common sense returned. "I am past the age of worrying about such things. But I thank you for your concern. And I shall do what I can to contain Mama. For Dezzie's sake, of course."

"Of course," he replied. And bowing again, he followed his mama to the brougham.

Mama and Aunt Hortense immediately went to discussing the visit. And Dezzie complained, though in a whisper so Mama could not hear, "Licia, what a Banbury tale! Me! Interested in land reform."

But Licia heard little of anything around her. She was lost in remembering a pair of dark eyes and a quizzical smile. And of course it had been most enlightening to talk to a man whose ideas were so progressive.

2

"Mama is quite wrong," said Dezzie with a prodigious sigh. "How can she ever think the duke would make a good husband? Why, his own mama has declared he doesn't believe in marriage!"

The young women had gathered in Penelope's room before dinner. Licia sighed. With Mama elsewhere, deciding what to wear, Dezzie felt free to speak her mind. And that was usually far from enlightening.

Dezzie was getting more difficult to reason with. Alas, she seemed to be growing more and more like Mama.

"His grace is not a bad sort," Penelope observed from her place on the chaise longue. "He makes sense when he talks." She cast Licia an amused look that said Dezzie often did not. "Yes, his grace knows what he's about."

Dezzie tossed her golden head, to the imminent danger of her artfully arranged curls. "Oh, he knows, all right. But he knows all the wrong things!"

Penelope gave her cousin a comforting smile. "I shouldn't worry, Dezzie, dear. I don't think even your mama can prevail upon Ravenworth to do what he doesn't wish to do."

Dezzie seemed much relieved by this and went off to admire the various bottles and jars that inhabited her cousin's vanity table.

"Does his grace have such a reputation, then?" Licia inquired, shifting a little uncomfortably in her lyre-back chair.

Penelope shrugged. "Every fashionable mama in London

has set her daughter's cap for him. And every last one has failed."

Licia swallowed a smile. Strange that such news should make her feel like smiling. But of course she was thinking of Dezzie, who would be dreadfully unhappy with such a man.

"They say he'll never marry," Penelope continued. "In fact, I've heard that even the worst wagerers at White's refuse to put money on it."

"And what do you think?"

Penelope smoothed the skirt of her lavender gown. "I think he may change his mind. People do, you know. People who were once firmly against matrimony decide that it is just the thing for them."

Since Penelope had been one of those very people, vowing that she would never marry, Licia hastened to ask, "And what makes them change their minds so emphatically?"

Penelope smiled again. "Love, of course. When you fall in love, everything changes."

Penelope's usually pale cheeks took on a pinkish hue, and her plain face seemed to glow. Licia reached out to touch her cousin's hand. "Do you mean that—"

"What's in this bottle?" Dezzie asked, thrusting a delicate cut-glass vial before Penelope's eyes.

"It's a new scent Mama purchased for me. I don't care for it."

Dezzie sighed dramatically. "I cannot understand these young women who don't value the accoutrements of social life."

Her tone was so like Mama's that Licia exchanged an amused glance with her cousin. But when Penelope raised an eyebrow and looked about to give way to laughter, Licia warned her with a slight shake of her head. Dezzie did not mimic Mama on purpose. The poor child did it quite without knowing it. And, if called to account, she would vehemently deny it.

"So," said Dezzie, absently fingering the bottle, "what sort of gentlemen are about in London?"

"All sorts," said Penelope.

Dezzie frowned. "Just so they aren't like Ravenworth. He's so infernally sober."

Recalling the duke's exact tone as he repeated the word *muddy*, Licia had hard work not to break into laughter. But she restrained herself. Dezzie, like Mama, had no appreciation of the more subtle forms of humor. And now was not the time to explain things. Besides, Dezzie had already taken a dislike to the duke. Bringing her to think more kindly of him would serve no good purpose.

Dezzie picked up Penelope's bonnet and set it on her curls. Standing there before the cheval glass, she turned this way and that, admiring her reflection. Then she put the bonnet back on a chair. "I shall know the gentleman for me. When I see him, I shall know him."

Penelope smiled. "I've no doubt of that, my dear. In the end, love is all."

"Love," repeated Dezzie with a look of artificial rapture that almost broke Licia's tenuous restraint on laughter.

"I think," she told her sister, "that your hair is becoming a bit untidy. Perhaps you'd better go ask Martha to have a look at it."

Dezzie's hands flew to her curls. "Oh, yes. Right away. I'll see you at dinner." And out she scurried.

Licia heaved a sigh of relief and turned to her cousin. "Now, my dear, what is all this stuff and nonsense about love?"

Penelope smiled. There was something strange and misty about her eyes. "It's true. Ravenworth taught me that."

"Ravenworth?" Why had her stomach taken this unaccountable desire to turn somersaults? It felt like a troupe of acrobats had taken up residence there.

"You see," Penelope continued, "our mamas meant us for each other." She sighed. "Yes, I know it seems strange now. After all, I am no beauty."

"Perhaps not, but—"

Penelope's smile was golden. "Don't, Cousin. I know I am plain. It no longer signifies. But you wanted to hear about Ravenworth . . ."

Licia was nodding before she quite realized it. "That is," she amended, "I wish to hear more on this subject of love."

"Of course." Penelope's tone was suspiciously like that of the duke during his conversation with Mama, but her face gave no hint of amusement. "Well," she went on, "our mamas meant us for each other. And the dear duchess treated me like a daughter. But David and I saw early on that it wouldn't suit. We do care for each other, of course."

Licia experienced another riot in the vicinity of her stomach. The acrobats were executing all their routines at once.

"But," Penelope went on, "it is as brother and sister. We grew up together and we are very affectionate."

"Then I don't see—"

Penelope laced her fingers together. "It takes more than affection to make a marriage work, my dear. David taught me that. And oh, he was so right. Love is—" She seemed to recollect herself and broke off. "So he and I made a pact. We simply both withstood our mamas."

Licia gazed at her cousin in awe. "You withstood *your* mama!" Aunt Hortense was a veritable dragon, not a scatterbrain like Mama.

Penelope nodded. "It was frightening, I assure you. But

21

David stood firm and so did I. And eventually they realized the inevitable."

"But should you not have liked being the Duchess of Ravenworth?" For some strange reason such a prospect made Licia's heart beat faster.

Penelope laced and unlaced her fingers. "More than any other thing, I desire to be loved. Loved in the way a man should love a woman. And David could not love me that way." Penelope lowered her voice. "He has had many women. After all, he's a lord. But I venture to say that he has never loved a one of them."

This news left Licia feeling a trifle light-headed. "And that," she finally ventured, "is why he is still unmarried?"

Penelope nodded. "Yes. And he will stay that way until the right woman comes along."

This possibility proved so intriguing to Licia's errant thoughts that she quite forgot to inquire any further into the reasons for Penelope's changed attitude toward love or the new rosiness to her cheeks.

The next afternoon found the three young women setting out for Bond Street. As they left the house in Grosvenor Square, Licia could hardly believe they were unattended by Mama. "How did you ever contrive this?" she asked her cousin.

Penelope's color grew higher, but her voice was steady. "Actually it was Mama's idea. She was afraid that your mama . . . that is . . ."

"I quite understand. So we have been deputized to choose Dezzie's gown."

Penelope nodded. "And gowns for ourselves."

"Your mama has great confidence in your ability," Licia said.

Penelope frowned. "In the matter of clothes, Mama has great confidence in me. In other matters . . ." She shrugged.

Licia wished to pursue these interesting "other matters." But Dezzie inquired, "What's that girl doing over there?"

"She's selling flowers," Penelope said.

Dezzie laughed. "How odd. At home we should just go out and pick some."

"Yes, of course, dear," said Licia. "But we are in the city now. And flowers do not grow wild and free."

"Indeed," observed Penelope. "Nothing in the city is free."

The carriage stopped before the modiste's establishment. "I'll just wait here, miss," said the coachman.

Penelope nodded.

Licia allowed herself to look around. There was indeed a great deal to see. The city teemed with life. But she was conscious of a vague disappointment.

Beside her, Dezzie asked, "We shan't see *him*, shall we?"

"Who, dear?"

"Ravenworth, of course."

"You should not be afraid of the duke," said Licia. "He will do you no harm."

Dezzie tossed her head. It was becoming one of her favorite and most affected gestures. "I'm not afraid of him anymore. He's just so dreadfully dull."

"Dezzie, how can you . . ." Licia paused. "That is, his grace is a very interesting conversationalist, but I can understand why you might wish for lighter topics."

She was not surprised to discover, however, that she herself would be pleased to continue their discussion about land reform. *Or about anything else,* whispered a small voice.

But Licia gave that voice no credence. It was perfectly natural to wish for more conversation such as she had enjoyed with the duke. She missed Papa and their discussions. It was pleasant to use her intellect again. And it was pleasant to see the duke smile.

Enough, she told herself. She was past the age of hanging out for a husband. And even if she were not, Ravenworth was beyond her reach. How fortunate Penelope was—to have him for a lifelong friend. If only she . . .

But the same nagging little voice informed her that though lifelong had a nice ring to it where the duke was concerned, friend was not the word she wished to have follow it.

"Licia," said Penelope, and it was evidently not for the first time. "Do stop your woolgathering. We have much work to do."

And work they did, emerging more than an hour later, tired but triumphant. "I think they will serve quite well," Penelope said.

"Yes," Licia agreed. "But I don't see why you insisted on such a gown for yourself. The color is all wrong. It doesn't show you to advantage."

"This is not my come-out."

"But still—"

Penelope's eyes grew hard. "Licia, dear, I appreciate your concern. But please believe me. I know what I am doing."

She glanced around her. "Perhaps Dezzie would like to walk a little. See the sights. Parker can follow us with the coach."

"Yes, of course." There was clearly no sense saying any more about it. But why had Penelope deliberately set out to make herself less attractive?

"Licia, look!" Dezzie cried. "Here's the most delightful bonnet. And look there."

Licia looked. And so with much looking and exclaiming on Dezzie's part, they made their way along Bond Street.

But unlike her sister, Licia found herself far more interested in the people than in the shop window displays. While Dezzie exclaimed over bonnets and ribbons, Licia enjoyed the dandies in their shining boots and high cravats, the ladies in their gaily colored gowns and pelisses.

It was not until sometime later, when a gentleman smiled at her, that she realized what she was doing. She jerked her glance away immediately and the gentleman passed on. But he did not take with him the rather disturbing knowledge that she had been scrutinizing the faces of passing gentlemen for the features of one particular man. She'd been searching the crowd for the Duke of Ravenworth.

It was ridiculous, of course, to hope to find one man in such a press of people. But beyond that, it was quite disturbing. Why, when he was clearly not the man for Dezzie, had the duke stayed so much in her thoughts? It was a question she could not answer and this was not the place to discuss it with Penelope.

Dezzie stopped to admire a display of half-boots and Licia caught herself, turning again to look for *him*. He was not there, of course. But a youngish man was going by and he glanced her way. At first she thought his smile was meant for her. But then, turning indignantly away, she got a look at Penelope's face. Her cousin was smiling back—with such love and tenderness that it was apparent the young man meant a great deal to her.

Licia turned back toward the crowd, determined to get another look, but he was almost out of sight. She could not remember much, just a general impression of shabbiness—a coat that did not quite fit and a cravat that was tied very plainly. "Penelope, who—"

With a glance at Dezzie, Penelope shook her head. "Later," she whispered.

★ ★ ★ ★ ★

But later seemed a long time in coming. As soon as they returned to Grosvenor Square, they must sit down to some refreshments. Licia, listening to Penelope describe the cut and color of each gown, marveled at her cousin's duplicity. Her glowing account made her own gown sound quite the most dazzling when actually . . . But perhaps Aunt Hortense wouldn't notice even when the gowns arrived. The striped puce-and-yellow creation she was wearing looked more appropriate for covering a chair than a matron. And even then . . .

"And then," concluded Dezzie, "we strolled along Bond Street."

Only Licia noticed the slight paling of her cousin's cheeks. But Penelope needn't have worried. Dezzie had seen nothing but the marvelous shop windows, the contents of which she now began to catalog.

Mama nodded complacently and observed, "I knew my decision to come to London was the right one." She fixed her elder daughter with a stern eye. "You were quite wrong, Licia, to go against me in this. You must see that now."

"Yes, Mama." Since the damage was done and they were already in the city, there seemed little use in defending herself. And besides, she was eager to get Penelope alone. To find out more about the shabby young man.

"I'm feeling . . ." she began but paused as Herberts entered the room.

"The Duke of Ravenworth," he announced.

Aunt Hortense looked a little surprised but she rallied. "And the dowager duchess?"

"No, milady. His grace is alone."

This information seemed difficult for Aunt Hortense to assimilate. But Penelope rose to the occasion. "Show his grace in."

"Yes, yes," echoed Aunt Hortense. "Show the man in."

The duke was looking his usual modish self. If anything, his boots shone even more brilliantly than they had the day before. But Licia no longer found his sartorial splendor offensive. He was a fine figure of a man. Why shouldn't his dress show it?

Penelope smiled at him and waved a hand. "Good afternoon, David. Have a seat and tell us why you are here."

Licia stared. How could Penelope talk to the man like that? As if he were the gardener or the butler?

But he only chuckled. "Of course, Pen. But I don't mean to stay long."

"I'm sure you're always welcome here," observed Mama with that sickeningly sweet smile.

His grace shrugged. "Of course, ma'am." He directed his look at Penelope, but somehow, in doing it, his glance crossed Licia's. She could not help herself—she smiled. And then, feeling foolish, she looked away again. He would think her as addlepated as Mama!

"I have come, Pen, to take you and your guests for a ride in the park. The fashionable hour approaches. And it will do Miss Desiree no harm to be seen out driving."

"Indeed," said Aunt Hortense, finally regaining the use of her tongue. "It will do her much good to be seen driving with *you*. As you well know."

He accepted the compliment with a complacent nod. "So, Pen, what do you say? Shall we show them Rotten Row?"

"We have been shopping all afternoon," Penelope began.

Licia's heart started a dangerous dance. Surely Penelope would not deny them this ride. She tried to think what she could say that would not be too forward.

But Dezzie didn't bother with such niceties. "I should like to go to the park," she said. "If it's full of people."

"It shall be," his grace promised. He turned then, his eyes meeting Licia's. "I hope Miss Dudley will find it entertaining too."

"No doubt I shall," she murmured, wondering if her cheeks were as rosy as they felt. "No doubt I shall."

3

The Duke helped Dezzie and Penelope into the front-facing seat so Dezzie could see as much as possible. He seated himself and Licia on the squabs that faced backward. It took a little getting used to, seeing where one had been instead of where one was going, but Licia soon forgot that in the wonder of looking around her.

Hyde Park was indeed full of people. Considering the press of carriages, Licia wondered that any of them could move. "Is it always like this?"

Ravenworth smiled. "Only from five onward. Earlier in the day it is quite deserted."

"Then I shall always come after five," declared Dezzie. "For I love to see the people." And she commenced to quiz Penelope about those passing by.

The duke raised an eyebrow. "Your sister seems to have taken to the city."

"Yes," Licia replied. "But she is so very young. And since she has never learned to ride, she has not had the opportunity to enjoy the countryside."

"My word! Never learned to ride! Have you no horses, then?"

"Oh, yes, we have horses." Now she'd gone and gotten herself in the suds again—made the family sound ever dottier than it was. "But Dezzie was afraid of them. And so Mama said she didn't have to learn."

"I see."

His tone spoke volumes—and all of them not to her liking.

"Mama is a little . . . flighty," she hurried to explain. "And by then Papa was gone."

His eyes softened. "And the management of family affairs fell upon your shoulders."

She did not even think of denying it. "Yes," she murmured. "And sometimes it is difficult. Though Mama is a dear, she can be so . . ."

The duke chuckled softly. "Determined?" he offered.

"Yes indeed." For some reason she found herself wanting to laugh. "You, Your Grace, have a wonderful facility with words."

He bowed slightly. "Thank you for the compliment. Though I am not sure I deserve it. Words are often quite inadequate for describing the curiosities of nature."

She had the uncomfortable feeling that he had classed Mama as one of those curiosities, and then she felt a twinge of disloyalty. But Mama *was* eccentric. Everyone at home said so.

"So," continued Ravenworth. "What do *you* think of the city?"

"I prefer the country. Since I like long rides and quiet days."

"You have not spent much time in the city."

She replied, "No, Papa loved the country. He said he only pursued business in order to live where he pleased. And he pleased to live in York."

"I wager your Mama was not so pleased."

"Mama loved Papa." She saw his look of surprise. "It's true. She married him when he was young and poor. For love. And he always had a way with her." She sighed. "I am not so fortunate. Or we should still be in York."

"That would be a pity." Something flickered in his eyes, something she did not understand.

She laughed. "Oh, yes, indeed. A real pity. Then all London should be spared the details of my . . . ah, introduction to life."

"She hasn't already—"

"No, Your Grace. So far I am safe. Unless, of course, someone has come to call while we are out."

The duke did not look pleased. "It's a shame Lady Hortense cannot keep her more in hand."

"I think she did when they were young. But now Mama has means. And she has always had determination. So we are here. And Dezzie will have a come-out that dazzles all London."

"And you . . ."

There was a softness to his voice that gave her a curious sort of feeling inside. "Why, I, Your Grace, shall go on as always."

"Why doesn't your Mama bring you both out?"

"Your Grace!" The blood flooded her cheeks. "How can you suggest that? I am far too old for such a thing."

"You don't look old to me." His voice had fallen another octave, and a curious sensation of warmth rushed through her limbs.

"You . . . you are most kind."

"Kindness has nothing to do with it."

This interesting statement hung in the air between them while Licia sought a reply. But before anything could come to mind, Dezzie leaned across and said, "Look, Licia, at that man over there. The one with the light-colored horses."

The duke leaned forward to get a better view, and the sleeve of his coat brushed that of Licia's pelisse. A curious weakness invaded her body as she, too, leaned to look.

"That is Prinny, the Prince Regent," Ravenworth explained. "Driving his Hanoverian creams. Some admirable cattle, those."

Dezzie fixed him with an accusing eye. "You are bamming me, Your Grace. That can't be the prince. He's too—"

The duke did not allow her to finish. "That *is* the Prince Regent," he said sternly. "And whatever adjective you were about to use is better left unsaid. Prinny is Prinny, and that's that."

Dezzie subsided, but she did not look convinced. And no wonder. The Prince Regent had obviously been eating to excess. Licia made a mental note to have a talk with Dezzie. Obviously it was not de rigueur to speak of the prince's corpulence.

"Ah," said the duke with such obvious satisfaction that all the women turned to look at him.

"There is my nephew, Viscount Lockwood. Pearsons, take us to my nephew."

Soon the carriage had pulled up beside a young man on horseback. "George," called the duke, "stop a minute. Over there."

The young man nodded and guided his horse off the roadway. The carriage followed.

Lockwood dismounted and came over to the carriage. He was a pale young man with curly blond locks and a look of such intense melancholy that Licia wondered if he suffered from some fatal illness.

"George," said the duke, "I want you to meet Pen's cousins. Miss Licia Dudley. Miss Desiree Dudley. This is my nephew, George, Viscount Lockwood."

"Pleased," said the viscount. His eyes went to Dezzie. "Very pleased. P'rhaps the ladies would like to get down. Promenade, you know."

"Oh, yes!" Dezzie got eagerly to her feet.

The duke cast an amused look at Licia before he said, "Well, Pen, do we have time?"

"I don't—"

"Oh, puh-lase," implored Dezzie in tones that almost reduced Licia to helpless laughter. It was unfair of Ravenworth to make sport of her, but Dezzie's reactions were amusing.

"Very well," said the duke. "We shall walk for a while. Perhaps, George, you'll give Miss Desiree your arm."

" 'Lighted," said that gentleman, and moved with alacrity to help Dezzie descend.

As the two moved off, chatting amiably, the duke offered his arms to his companions. "We'll just follow behind, as proper chaperons ought."

Licia tried to take in the sights, but she found leaning on his grace's arm strangely debilitating. In some odd fashion it seemed to interfere with her breathing.

"Well," said his grace to Penelope, "what do you think of George?"

"He looks like a washed-out copy of Byron. My word, David, where *did* he get those curls?"

The duke chuckled. "Probably the same place as his hero."

"You can't mean . . . Byron uses curl papers?"

"So I've heard."

Licia could remain silent no longer. "Please, are you saying that your nephew is aping the poet?"

"Yes," said his grace and Penelope together.

"But whatever for?"

Penelope laughed. "Really, Licia. Byron is all the rage with the ladies. His curls. His melancholy looks. And, of course, *Childe Harold*." She turned to the duke. "Has George taken up writing poetry?"

"I should hope not. I've no doubt he'd be dreadful at it."

He gazed after the two young people. "But Miss Desiree seems to find the boy quite admirable."

How could Dezzie prefer this pale young fop to the duke? Licia wondered. But it was just as well. Dezzie and the duke would never deal well together. He needed someone more mature, more sensible, more . . . This train of thought led her to some pleasant daydreams that occupied the rest of their short walk.

When they returned to the carriage, the viscount made his good-byes with evident regret, and Dezzie gazed after his departing figure with wide, admiring eyes. "Oh," she said to Ravenworth. "Your nephew is such an admirable man, and so learned. Why, he knew the names of all the persons we passed."

And then she subsided into a silence in which she gazed off into the crowd with sighs and dreamy looks of the most exquisite sensibility.

Some time later the duke left them at the door, and Dezzie, newly invigorated, rushed into the sewing room, discarding bonnet and pelisse as she went. "Oh, Mama, Hyde Park is so wonderful! We saw the Prince Regent and all the lords and ladies. And we met the duke's nephew."

"Ah, yes," said Aunt Hortense. "Young Lockwood. A bit of a—A nice young man."

"Yes, Mama," Licia added. "And the duke seems very fond of him."

Dezzie cast her a look of such impassioned gratitude that it was a wonder Mama didn't become immediately suspicious. But Mama was not too bright in some respects.

"Do you think," Dezzie began, "that since the duke's nephew is in town . . ." She hesitated, plainly afraid to go on.

Penelope stepped into the breach. "I'm sure David would

appreciate his nephew being invited to the ball. And as Mama says, the viscount is a fine young man."

Aunt Hortense looked about to speak but at a glance from her daughter remained silent.

Dezzie, too, said no more, but to Licia her agitation was so apparent, she wondered that Mama could not see it. As usual, Mama had other thoughts to occupy her. "Well," she said, "I suppose it would be the polite thing to do." She smiled. "We want to keep Dezzie's intended happy."

"Yes, Mama, we do." Licia grabbed Dezzie by the arm before she could speak and dragged her out the door. "Come, dear, let's go wash up."

"I won't marry the duke," Dezzie exclaimed as they reached the room she and Licia shared. "Why didn't you let me tell Mama so?"

"You have already told her. And she didn't hear you."

Penelope nodded. "Your sister is quite right. Besides, there is nothing to worry about. David is not the marrying kind. And no one, not even *your* mama, can persuade him to be otherwise." She paused in the doorway. "If you've a minute, Licia . . ."

"Oh, yes." Being with Ravenworth had quite driven out all other thoughts out of her mind. But now she was again wondering about that man who had smiled at Penelope.

"You freshen up, dear," she told Dezzie. "I'll be back shortly."

Dezzie nodded and sank down on the chaise. From the look of her she was already lost in dreams of the melancholy young viscount.

Licia hurried down the hall beside her cousin. "Who—"

But Penelope shook her head. "Not here."

Once they were safely inside Penelope's room, the door

closed behind them, Licia grabbed her cousin by the arm. "Now, Penelope. You must tell me now. Who is he?"

Penelope's smile was beautiful. Her whole face glowed with it and her eyes turned soft and misty. "He's the most wonderful man in the world. And he loves me."

Licia settled herself into a chair. "But who is he? You must tell me all."

"His name is Harry Bates. And he's a painter."

"A . . . painter?"

"Don't look at me like that. He's studying painting with Turner. On Queen Anne's Street."

It was plain that Penelope cared a great deal for this man. But even in York one learned that ladies of good family did not marry artists. Licia sighed. "It must be fine to be loved. But your mama—"

Penelope's expression sobered. "Mama doesn't know." Catching Licia's expression of dismay, she hurried on. "Oh, I know how she'll respond. So we are waiting. To see if Harry can make a name for himself."

Much as it pained her, Licia had to say it. "I don't think—"

"Neither do I. But Harry says we must try. He wants to do the right thing. And above all, he does not want Mama to think him a fortune hunter!"

"But she will! How can she not?" Licia took a deep breath. For Penelope's sake the question must be asked. "Are you quite sure he is not?"

Fortunately Penelope did not bristle. She was too level-headed to fly up in the boughs. "Yes, I am sure. When you know him, you will be sure too. I would have taken you to the gallery today. But with Dezzie along . . ."

Licia's head was spinning. Imagine Penelope in love! After all these years. "How did you meet?"

"Mama sent me for a painting. We saw Turner's work at

the Royal Academy. He does the most marvelous things with storms. And sunlight." She smiled. "When I went to the gallery to inquire, Turner was out. And Harry talked to me."

She settled on a nearby chair. "He is so different from most men of my acquaintance. There's not a bit of the dandy or the fop about him."

Thinking of the shabbiness she had glimpsed, Licia could only nod.

"He's a dutiful son too. He sends money to his mama." She sighed. "I know you will think me strangely befuddled, but I *know* I should be happy anywhere with my dear Harry. But he . . . he wants us to wait till he can better support me. Can you imagine? He doesn't want to take my dowry."

"But how shall you live?"

Penelope shook her head. "I don't know. But I shall not give him up. He's the first man I've ever known that made me consider matrimony a blessing."

Licia thought for a moment. Her cousin's happiness was evident, and Penelope, even in love, was a good judge of character. But this was a real problem. "Is there no one to whom you can turn for help?"

Penelope shook her head. "No one else knows. You are the first to be told. And for heaven's sake, don't let Dezzie know."

"Of course not. But why haven't you told Ravenworth? I thought you said you were friends."

Penelope sighed. "Yes, we are. But Ravenworth is a peer. He cannot be expected to understand this. And beyond that, he holds no belief for love. He would simply tell me to stop acting the green girl."

This information gave Licia a most disconcerting feeling. "But I thought he had not married because he had found no one he could love."

"That is my belief. And his mama's. But David *says* he does not believe in the institution of marriage."

There was no reason this news should leave her feeling so dispirited. After all, she did not want him to marry Dezzie.

"You must promise not to tell a living soul," Penelope went on. "Mama must not find out too soon. It would ruin everything."

"I would never tell Dezzie. Like Mama, she cannot keep anything a secret. But I think you are wrong about Ravenworth."

"Promise," Penelope commanded. "Not a single word."

Licia bowed to the inevitable. "You have my word. Oh, dear, I wish I could help."

"Perhaps you can. I have been going far too often to the gallery. Perhaps sometimes you may carry a message for me."

The prospect was not thrilling. Clandestine liaisons could only lead to disaster. But Licia nodded. She could do no less for the friend of her childhood. Sighing, she settled back in her chair. "So tell me all about your Harry."

4

Several days passed, days that seemed singularly empty without Ravenworth's company. And then early one afternoon while they were all sitting at their needlepoint and Mama was elaborating on her plans for Dezzie's come-out, Herberts entered to announce, "The Duke of Ravenworth. The dowager duchess. And her friend, the Duchess of Oldenburgh."

Mama's eyes lit up. Dukes and duchesses were her favorite people. English or Russian, French or German, these details made no difference to her. In her view, nobility was made to be cultivated. "My dear duchess," Mama cooed, "do come sit by me." She stroked the sable wrap the duchess wore. "Tell me about those dreadful Russian winters. I hear that they are so very cold."

To Licia the duchess did not look particularly noble. There was a strange cast to her features—an un-English flatness that made her seem indeed quite foreign.

While the ladies were fussing over her, the duke took a chair near Licia. She experienced a brief fluttering on her heart but resolutely put it down. Such reactions were for green girls, not for women of her age.

Then, finding the duke's eyes upon her, she searched her mind for something to say. "Dezzie has talked so often of our drive in Hyde Park. Thank you again for taking us."

What a stupid way to open a conversation. She was getting as bad as Mama, practically asking him to take them for a drive again.

But Ravenworth didn't seem to mind. "The pleasure was

all mine," he said politely. He shifted his gaze to Mama then back to her. "Your mama seems to find the duchess quite charming. Has she a penchant for things foreign?"

"Not exactly," Licia replied. "It is more likely that she has a penchant for things noble."

The duke absorbed this information with a dry laugh. "No doubt."

In the silence that followed, Licia heard Mama say, "It was truly the most magnificent bed. Twelve feet long and eight feet wide, with the most lovely decorated dome. And figures that played the most marvelous, most delightful music."

The duke pulled in a breath. "My word, don't tell me she's—"

Licia sighed. "I'm afraid she is."

"But I distinctly told her . . ."

Though the situation could hardly be classed as humorous, Licia swallowed a sudden urge to giggle. Ravenworth looked so startled. No doubt few people had ever dared to cross him. Unfortunately he would find Mama a different story.

"Mama only hears what she wishes to hear," she explained. "You cannot expect her to forgo telling the story of the Celestial Bed. Aside from running off with Papa, it was the most romantic event in her life."

He frowned. "She ran off with him? What a fool thing to do."

She could hardly disagree with that. Runaway marriages *were* most often disastrous. Still, Mama was *her* mama. "Perhaps. I thought I had told you that."

He shook his head. "You told me she loved him. I thought the family had come round."

"No indeed. They ran off and Mama's family disowned her. But then, when Papa became successful, they relented.

So when we were girls, Penelope used to come visit in the summer."

He nodded. "She told me how much she enjoyed those visits. Tell me, do you find her much changed?"

Her heart rose up in her throat. Careful. She must be careful with Penelope's precious secret. "Changed? How?"

He adjusted his cuff. "I don't know exactly. I can not quite put a finger on it. She's just different somehow."

She let herself relax a little. He didn't really know anything. "You must remember that I haven't seen her for several summers, so it's hard to say. But she seems like herself to me."

The duke frowned. "There's something different. I know it."

"My dear duke," said Mama, smiling at him from across the room.

"Yes, Mrs. Dudley?"

Licia felt the hair rising on the back of her neck. That was the tone Mama used when she wanted something from a man.

"How is the weather today?"

Ravenworth looked a little bewildered but he replied, "The sun was shining when we arrived."

"How excellent! My dear Dezzie has been languishing for want of fresh air. And now the sun is shining."

She stared at him pointedly. But either Ravenworth was stunned by this frontal attack or he had determined to ignore it.

While he sat there, still silent, his mama intervened. "The duchess and I should like to make this a longer visit. Perhaps, David, you could take the young ladies out for a drive."

"As you wish, Mama," he said dutifully.

Licia, who had no desire to be foisted on the man, opened

her mouth to protest. But a look from Penelope caused her to close it again without saying a single word. For some reason Penelope wished to take this drive.

Licia ventured a glance at the duke. His face remained quite expressionless. But there! By his mouth the muscle was twitching again. He must think them a veritable raree-show!

She fumed while they got their wraps, but once settled in the carriage with Ravenworth beside her and the spring sun peeping through the clouds, she found it quite impossible to be upset.

"I must say, David," Penelope observed in a chafing tone, "that you were dreadfully slow to put your carriage at our disposal."

He smiled, not at all disturbed. "Since you are as well equipped as I in the carriage line, I had no idea Miss Desiree was wilting away."

"I am afraid Mama is rather transparent," Licia said. "I must ask you to forgive her."

The duke frowned. "I can forgive her for maneuvering me into something I am quite willing to do. But the story of that horrendous bed . . . Is there no way to stop her?"

Licia suppressed an urge to pat his hand. She must remember he was not Dezzie, to be comforted with a pat. "I'm afraid not. But do not fret. I have grown used to it."

His frown deepened. "Used to it, indeed. The details of one's . . ."

"Introduction to life," she supplied helpfully, wondering why she was almost overwhelmed by a desire to laugh.

"Thank you." The man actually glowered. "Such intimate details ought not to be public knowledge."

"Quite true," agreed Licia. "But since Aunt Hortense and Penelope and I and your mama—and even you—have failed to make an impression on Mama, there seems little more we can do."

"Licia is quite right," said Penelope. "Tell me, David, have you time to drive us to Queen Anne's Street?"

Licia caught her breath. That was the place of Turner's gallery. What was Penelope planning?

"And what do you fancy there?" Ravenworth asked pleasantly.

"Mama is considering purchasing a Turner. And I am commissioned to choose it. I could use your advice on the matter."

"Certainly. If the others have no objections."

And since there were none, he instructed his driver to set off.

"So," said Ravenworth, "what do you think of our Russian guest?"

Penelope shrugged. "She seems right enough. But do all their nobility have that curious flatness to the features?"

Dezzie giggled. "I heard her say that someone had referred to her as platter-faced. Isn't that apt?"

Before Licia could remonstrate with her, Ravenworth turned a stern gaze on the culprit. "Whoever said that was unkind. And whoever repeats it . . ." He paused significantly. "Whoever repeats it is foolish and a troublemaker to boot. Do you understand?"

For a moment Dezzie looked rebellious. But then, evidently deciding it was wisest to exercise caution, she nodded. "Of course I understand. I am not a gossipmonger."

Licia almost choked on the laugh she swallowed. Then she leaned back on the squabs and smiled to herself. If Ravenworth could not change Dezzie, he was at least having a civilizing influence on her. She only hoped it would continue.

★ ★ ★ ★ ★

The gallery was a cluttered place, with pictures everywhere—hanging frame to frame or leaning against each other in a most haphazard fashion. Licia recognized the man who stepped forward to greet them.

So this was Harry Bates. His clothes were indeed shabby and plain, but they were also clean and neat. His smile, because of the others present, was carefully reserved. But there was a friendliness to it that Licia believed might always be in evidence. She liked the man already. Surely such a man could not be a fortune hunter.

"Good day, Lady Penelope," he said.

Penelope nodded and, with just the right touch of haughtiness, replied, "Good day, Mr. Bates. I've brought the duke to help me decide which painting to purchase for Mama."

Ravenworth looked from one to the other, and Licia held her breath. If he should suspect something amiss . . .

But Ravenworth only nodded. "I've long been an admirer of Turner's technique."

And then the front door opened again. Licia heard Dezzie's sharp intake of breath. And the Viscount Lockwood said, "Ravenworth, old chap! I saw your carriage and . . ." He paused and bowed. "Afternoon ladies."

Dezzie cast him a melting smile. "Good afternoon, milord. Isn't it a lovely day?"

"Capital," declared the young man. He ran a hand through his riot of curls. "Even better since I've seen you."

Dezzie dimpled. "Tell me, milord, are you conversant with Mr. Turner's techniques?"

"Well, I guess I know somewhat."

Dezzie's smile grew. "Then perhaps you could explain to me how he gets some of his effects. Take this picture over here."

And while Licia watched in astonishment, Dezzie slipped

44

her arm through the viscount's and led him off.

With an amused smile Ravenworth turned to Harry Bates. "Perhaps you'll show us the scenes Lady Penelope is considering."

Bates nodded. "The first is over here."

Licia was interested in the effects Turner achieved with paint and brush. But even more fascinating was watching Penelope and Harry play out their charade. Harry seemed a little nervous, but then that could be attributed to the presence of a duke in the establishment. And Penelope . . . why, Penelope could have gone upon the stage! In every particular she played the part of the highborn lady.

Ravenworth examined several paintings and asked questions that made it clear he was no novice in the matter of appreciating art. Finally he turned back to Penelope. "I suppose it comes down to whether your mama prefers storms over land or storms over sea." He looked to Licia. "Which is your preference, Miss Dudley?"

Since her mind had been far from the thought of paintings and her eyes had been following Dezzie and Lockwood as they moved about the gallery, it took her a moment to reply. Fortunately her gaze lit on a nearby canvas and she pointed to it.

"I like this one. *Frosty Morning*. Not that Mr. Turner's storms aren't marvelous. But I prefer peace and tranquillity. The quiet of country life. This scene is so peaceful. And the frost seems so real. It reminds me of home."

The duke nodded. "I, too, admire that effect."

For a moment his eyes looked directly into hers. They gave her such a feeling of giddiness that she almost reached out for something to cling to for support.

The feeling was disconcerting enough. But even more disturbing was the scene that her mind insisted on presenting her—a cozy domestic scene in which Ravenworth sat, his long legs stretched toward the fire while she listened to the results of his newest land reform. That picture left her decidedly giddy.

She looked away and his gaze went to Penelope. "Tell me if I'm wrong, Pen," he said. "But I collect Lady Chester wishes for a storm."

Penelope, who had been gazing at Harry Bates, looked quickly back to the duke. "Yes, David. Mama has decided she simply must have one of Turner's talked-about storms."

The duke looked from one painting to another. "Then I should take *Hannibal and His Army Crossing the Alps*. Though I confess that I should like to see a little more of Hannibal and his army and a little less of the storm."

Penelope nodded. "I like that one too. But I also like *Calais Pier*—the effect of the sun breaking through the storm clouds and gleaming on the water seems so real."

Harry Bates smiled just a little. "Of course, milady. That is a beautiful effect."

The way he pronounced the word *beautiful* sent little shivers down Licia's spine. It was plain—at least to her—that the word was meant for Penelope and not for any painting. And seeing the slight coloring of her cousins's cheeks, Licia knew Penelope thought so too. But a glance at Ravenworth convinced her he was oblivious.

Penelope considered both pictures and then shook her head. "I'm afraid I shall have to give the matter some more thought. You understand, Mr. Bates."

"Of course, milady."

Licia smiled to herself. Of course the decision would necessitate many more visits to the gallery.

Ravenworth called to his nephew. "Come, Lockwood. We are leaving now."

The duke turned away and so did Licia, but not before she saw Penelope slip a note into Harry Bates's outstretched hand.

Hurrying after the others, Licia tried to keep her expression serene. But Penelope's behavior was startling. True, she was no longer a young miss. But this kind of thing was still dangerous. If Ravenworth ever discovered her secret—or her mama—Licia shuddered to think what Aunt Hortense would have to say about such a disreputable liaison.

Young Lockwood accompanied them to the carriage where with a heavy sigh Dezzie withdrew her arm from his and allowed him to assist her to her seat. After which she bestowed on him a smile of bewitching magnitude and said, "Thank you for a most pleasurable time."

"Quite welcome," replied the young man with a matching smile. And with a sigh he took himself off to his curricle.

When they were once more moving homeward, the duke turned to Penelope and smiled. "Are you sure you are well? I have never known you to take so long in making up your mind about a thing."

Penelope shrugged. But she looked a little uncomfortable. "With so many to choose from, the choice is difficult. And, after all, it is not myself I have to please."

Ravenworth looked about to pursue the matter further. But Dezzie leaned toward him. "Mama says you were once intended to marry Cousin Penelope. Why did you not do it?"

Licia gasped. "Dezzie! Oh, dear! You must not—"

The duke laid a gloved hand over Licia's, and the ensuing sensation so bemused her that she fell immediately silent.

"You are quite right, Miss Desiree. Our mamas wished us to wed. *They* wished it to be true. But *we* did not."

Dezzie shook her golden head. "When *my* mama wishes something to be true, it *happens*."

Ravenworth frowned. Perhaps he was thinking of Mama's various impositions on his time. "Perhaps," he observed dryly, "but your mama is now in the city. And things are different here."

5

The night of Dezzie's ball finally arrived. After a day of immense confusion in which Mama continually found fault with everyone and everything, she sent them all off to dress.

Dezzie fluttered around the bedchamber like a distraught moth until Licia finally protested. "My dear, you must settle somewhere. You'll be exhausted before the ball begins."

Dezzie's eyes widened and she came to a stop in front of her sister. "But I am afraid. What if he doesn't come?"

"Who is this he?" Licia asked, though she knew quite well to whom Dezzie was referring.

Dezzie stared at her. "Why, the viscount, of course. The Viscount Lockwood." She clasped her hands in a gesture of despair. "If he doesn't like my gown, I shall die!"

Licia hid a smile. "Dezzie, my dear—"

"It's true." Dezzie fixed her sister with a look of the utmost intensity. "Lockwood is my intended. I know it."

"Dezzie, you've only just met the man. Talked to him twice."

Dezzie shook her head. "He's the one. I know it. When he looks at me . . . when he speaks to me . . . oh, Licia, my heart palpitates till I think it will quite fly out of my mouth!"

Licia swallowed another smile. Perhaps Dezzie was in the right. After all, what experience had her older sister in affairs of the heart? "And do you think he returns your regard?"

"Oh, I think so. I thought so. Oh, I don't know!" Dezzie wrung her hands in a manner that would have done honor to the renowned Mrs. Siddons. "How does a woman tell these things?"

Licia sighed. Unaccountably the situation had lost its humor. "I'm sorry, my dear. I cannot help you with this. But cheer up. I'm sure the viscount will put in an appearance. And who knows—after you have seen him again you may decide you prefer some other young man."

Dezzie's eyes widened in horror. "Never! Never!" she averred. "Lockwood is the one." She sighed. "Being in love is dreadfully trying. I should never have imagined how difficult it can be." She pulled at a ribbon. "Do you think I look all right?"

"My dear, you are beautiful." And it was true. In her gown of white satin trimmed with pale blue ribbons, matching ribbon threaded through her golden curls, and blue satin slippers peeking out from below the gown, Dezzie was a vision of loveliness. And Licia was not looking at her through sisterly eyes. When the young men saw Dezzie . . . Licia smiled. The viscount was in for a lot of competition.

She adjusted her own tunic dress of sea-foam sarcenet. It was the first gown she'd had edged with a Grecian motif, and she did think she looked rather well in it. But would he think it attractive? Or would he think she was addlepated, a spinster playing at going to the ball?

With a frown at such foolishness she turned from the cheval glass. She'd better get herself in hand. It mattered very little whether or not Ravenworth liked her gown. She was not there to be danced with and admired. She was a mere appendage to Dezzie's night of triumph. And she would do well to remember that. "Come," she told her sister, "let us go up to the ballroom."

The huge room had been decked out with potted palms and banks of blossoms till it resembled a greenhouse. But

Licia had to admit that it looked very festive and quite fashionable.

Mama, in a gown that was far too young for her, flitted around the room, her golden curls bobbing as she made a last-minute inspection of things.

"There you are," Aunt Hortense said, turning from the refreshment table. "You're both looking lovely."

"You're looking quite well yourself," Licia replied. And Aunt Hortense did look well. It was that abominable excuse for a gown in cerise and yellow striped taffeta that looked so sickening.

Surveying this creation of dubious merit, Licia understood how Penelope could choose the gown she had. Its yellow hues did nothing for her complexion, and the design of the gown, gathered tight under the bosom and then falling in a skirt that looked like nothing so much as a sausage casing, did nothing for her figure, either.

Penelope smiled and whispered. "Isn't this gown horrendous? It's just what I wanted. And Mama won't even know."

"Why—" began Licia.

But just then Mama came up. She fussed over the placement of Dezzie's curls, the hang of her ribbons, till Aunt Hortense exclaimed, "Upon my word, Dorothea. Leave the poor child alone. You'll only make her nervous with all that fuss."

Mama bristled, her blues eyes beginning to blaze. "I hope I may fix my own daughter's hair. On this most important night in her life." She drew herself up. "I knew I should never have—"

"Mama." Licia intervened before Mama could get well under way with her tirade. "Please do not scowl so. Remember, all must go well for Dezzie's sake. And just think, the guests will be arriving at any minute."

And arrive they did. One after the other till the ballroom seemed filled to overflowing. Licia watched as Dezzie grew ever more fidgety. "He will be here," she whispered, not certain if the reassurance was meant for herself or for Dezzie.

Fortunately she did not have time to give the matter much more thought. For there, through the crush, came the Duke of Ravenworth. And right beside him strode the Viscount Lockwood, resplendent in evening clothes and a white satin waistcoat shot with blue thread.

"Your servant," said Lockwood, bowing over Dezzie's hand rather longer than necessary.

She dimpled and curtsied and made quite the fool of herself. But the viscount didn't seem to care. And Mama thought all the attention was for the duke.

"Good evening," Ravenworth said to Licia. "You are looking well tonight."

Licia felt the warmth flooding her limbs. "So are you," she said. "Very well." As indeed he was. There were probably few men in London with a better leg than that revealed by his evening breeches and stockings.

There was something about his eyes—a warmth, a friendliness—that pleased her immensely. But then she reminded herself that the man himself pleased her. For a moment she allowed herself to enjoy the feeling.

And then, of course, Mama had to ruin it. "You must get your name on Dezzie's card immediately," she said to the duke. "I'm sure she'll want to have several dances with you."

The duke bowed, and while Licia watched in embarrassment he dutifully put himself down for a dance. Then he turned to Licia. "Where is your card, Miss Dudley?"

"I'm afraid I have none."

"Then will you honor me with the first dance?"

Though his request took her quite by surprise, it took her

only a moment to regain her senses. And she was able to reply with a smile. "Of course, Your Grace. If you wish it."

His smile warmed her. "Yes, I wish it."

Fortunately Mama soon decided that they no longer needed to stand to welcome people. So when the orchestra struck up and the duke appeared at her side, Licia was free to put her hand in his.

They danced the quadrille with great enjoyment, at least on her part. And when they had finished and he returned with her to the sidelines, he lingered to talk. "I, ah, do not quite know how to say this," he began.

Her heart fluttered under the new gown. "Oh, dear. It's the bed. The story has already spread."

His smile stopped her. "No, Miss Dudley. It is not the bed."

She heaved a sigh of relief. "Then what is it?"

"It's the waltz."

She was confused. "I'm sorry, I don't understand."

"Knowing your mama . . ." He coughed delicately and seemed to be considering how to continue. "Let me put it like this. I am afraid she may insist on the orchestra playing a waltz. And that would be folly."

She might have known. It was always Mama. It would be a miracle if they survived this season without some terrible slander besmirching their name. "The waltz? Is that the new dance?"

He nodded. "From Germany. The patronesses of Almack's are against it. They do not permit it to be danced in their rooms. And they set the fashion."

"I understand. I have not heard Mama mention it. But surely Aunt Hortense would tell her—"

The duke sighed. "Knowing your mama as I do, I seriously doubt if she would consult with your aunt. If someone requests a waltz"—he looked out over the crowd—"as some young buck well may, she will simply instruct the orchestra to play one."

"Oh, dear. Now what shall I do? Sometimes Mama can be very trying."

His smile was comforting. "A notion occurs to me. If you would be willing to leave the matter in my hands?"

How could she be otherwise? "Oh, yes. Most willing."

"Then excuse me while I attend to something."

He disappeared into the crowd, but not before a startling realization came to her. She would gladly have put any matter, including her own life, into his hands. It was a sobering thought, but she had no time to reflect on it, for Penelope pushed her way through the crush, closely followed by a portly, florid-faced man of middle years. And neither seemed particularly to be enjoying the other's company.

"There you are, Licia." Penelope took hold of her arm as though she'd found a rescuer. But the portly man stopped too.

"Your cousin?" he inquired, looking from one young woman to the other.

"Yes, Major. Major Fitzsimmons, my cousin, Miss Licia Dudley."

"Pleased to meet you," said the major in a voice that reflected absolutely no pleasure. "Dreadful crush, this. Don't like crowds."

Penelope laughed—a high, shrill sound so unlike her normal laughter that Licia was hard put not to stare at her. "Ta, major! What a stick you are. When I am wed, I shall hold a ball every week. With salmon patties and fresh ices and all the newest French cuisine."

The major's florid face took on a greenish hue. "Waste of funds. Terrible."

Penelope cackled again. There was no other word to describe the horrid sound. "Ha, when I wed, I shall waste all the funds I please. It will be the greatest fun."

The major shook his head. " 'Scuse me," he said. "I see an old friend over there. Really ought to talk to him."

As soon as he was out of earshot, Licia asked, "Penelope, whatever do you think you are doing?"

Penelope smiled. "I am protecting myself. I hear the major is hanging out for a wife. Unfortunately Mama heard too. That's why she invited him tonight. So I am endeavoring to protect myself in the best way I know."

Behind them, Ravenworth laughed. "And you think to do this by looking for all the world like a little sausage perched sideways on a big one?"

Penelope chuckled. "David, how dare you sneak up on us like that?"

He shrugged. "If I had asked outright, would you have told me the reason for this outlandish getup?"

"Of course not," Penelope said. "But speak softly. I don't want Mama to suspect."

The duke grimaced. "How can she not when you wear such a gown?"

Penelope tapped his arm with her fan. "You forget. Mama has no sense of fashion. One look at her should make that clear. And you know these dresses are now all the rage."

"And quite the ugliest things I've seen in an age."

"Quite so," agreed Penelope cheerfully. "And now, if you'll excuse me, I'm going to find the major and give him another good dose of married life. Perhaps that will be enough to discourage him altogether."

Ravenworth laughed. "I rather expect so."

Penelope was soon gone, and Ravenworth turned to Licia. "She's a resourceful girl, Pen is." The duke adjusted his cuffs. "She'll manage to elude this one." He turned his smile on Licia. "But tell me, how did you outwit your many suitors?"

He seemed determined to be kind to her. And she did not really mind answering his questions. It was always pleasant to talk to him. "It was very easy. I simply said no."

"And your mama did not protest?"

"No. You see, she was not eager to have me marry."

"Because that would leave everything upon her shoulders?"

She wanted to deny this, but she had never been good at lying. "Perhaps. It was a sad time—after Papa died. And for a while she needed someone to lean on. Truly I did not mind."

"There were none of these suitors that took your fancy?"

"No. I did not find the institution of marriage particularly appealing. Nor any of the men who proposed it. So I simply stayed home with my family."

"An admirable choice," he said with warmth. "The institution should be avoided."

"Perhaps." She wondered that she should go on with him in this fashion, but perversity drove her to say, "I have nothing against the institution itself. But I should wish to enter it with the right man."

A strange gleam came into his eyes. "And have you encountered such a man?"

Oh, dear. She felt the warmth flooding her limbs. How could she reply to such a question? But there he stood, waiting for an answer. "I . . . I am past the age of marrying."

"But—"

"Ravenworth." Lockwood appeared, tugging at the duke's sleeve. Ravenworth did not look pleased to be thus interrupted, but he said, "Yes?"

"We need your help. Miss Dezzie wishes to try the new waltz. And the orchestra will not comply. P'rhaps if you'd speak to them . . ."

Ravenworth fixed his nephew with a stern eye. "I have already spoken to them. And I assure you, they will *not* be playing a waltz."

Lockwood shifted uncomfortably. "But—"

"No buts," said the duke. "You know how Almack's patronesses are. Do you want to ruin the girl's chances altogether?"

"No, no. Course not." Lockwood pulled nervously at his cravat. "I'll tell her. I'll 'splain." And he scurried off.

Ravenworth sighed. "The boy means well. He just doesn't think." He offered her his hand. "These affairs are abominably slow. Shall we dance again?"

As they traced the steps of the quadrille Licia tried to think sensibly. Aunt Hortense and Penelope had both cautioned Dezzie. She might dance two dances with the same gentleman but no more. Even two dances might mean the gentleman held her in high regard. And more than that . . . more than that just wasn't done.

Of course, Ravenworth was not dancing with *her* because he held her in high regard. He was simply a kind and generous man. And he was looking out for Penelope's country cousin. But in spite of this sensible and undoubtedly true fact, her pleasure in the duke's company was quite untouched.

They finished the quadrille and stood again upon the sidelines, watching Lockwood and Dezzie tread a measure. As the two young people finished, Ravenworth said, "Excuse me. I believe this is my dance with your sister."

As the duke dutifully led Dezzie through the maneuvers of the dance, young Lockwood came to stand beside Licia. With his face flushed from the exertions of the dance and his eyes sparkling from whatever cause, he looked rather less melancholy than usual. He stood for several minutes before he said, "Miss Dudley, may I ask you a question?"

"Of course."

"I . . . that is . . . do you think . . . confound it!" He swallowed and tried again. "I'm wanting to ask you: Do you think Miss Dezzie might . . . might welcome my suit?"

Licia took pity on the boy. "I think she might."

He grabbed her hand and pumped it with great exuberance. "Oh, Miss Dudley. Thank you! You've made me so happy!"

"I only said *might,*" she reminded him. "And do not let on to Mama yet."

"Yes, yes. Thank you."

Watching him go, Licia sighed. They would have a hard time of it. Mama was determined that Dezzie land the duke. And she didn't care in the least that the duke had no wish to be landed.

"So," Ravenworth said, coming up behind her. "What was that all about?"

"What?"

"I saw my nephew beaming at you. And pumping your arm like—"

"Oh, he wanted to know if I thought Dezzie liked him."

"Just as I suspected. The boy is head over heels in love."

She waited for him to say more, but he remained silent. Finally, unable to restrain her curiosity, she inquired. "And what is your feeling on the matter?"

He smiled. "I think they suit each other."

This statement rather took her back. "You mean, you aren't against their marrying?"

"Of course not. The boy's been into his melancholy state far too long. With your sister around he couldn't possibly *stay* melancholy."

Licia absorbed this. "But I thought you were against the institution."

He shook his head. "Not for others. Only for myself. You see, I think it takes a certain sort of person, like you and I, to be able to function alone."

For some reason his compliment failed to make her feel pleasure. "But they're so young. Aren't you afraid they'll run amuck?"

"Not really. Underneath the patina of fashion the boy's really a sensible chap. I think they'll do quite well together." He frowned. "Of course, there's your mama to be considered. I collect she's aiming higher than a viscount."

Licia sighed. "I'm afraid so."

The evening passed far too rapidly to suit her. Ravenworth seemed to take the duties of friendship quite seriously. He spent much of the evening by her side while they engaged in the most pleasant conversation. So it was with some surprise that she heard the clock strike such a late hour.

She was trying to cope with a strong sensation of regret that this lovely evening would soon be ending when from beside her the duke uttered an exclamation of dismay. "That mutton-headed boy will ruin it all!"

He grabbed her hand. "Come. We must be quick."

"But we've already danced twice. We can't—"

He swung her expertly into the procession and whispered, "We must. With luck, the gossips will fix on us instead of your sister and my unthinking nephew. This is the third time he's danced with her."

"Oh." The prospect of becoming the topic of gossip was not at all to her liking, but there was Dezzie to think of. So she followed him through the steps, a false smile on her lips.

"People will not . . ." she began when the figure of the dance brought them together again. This whole incident was

59

most distressing to her. And trying to talk about it made her want to cry. But talk she must. She tried again. "I do not think people will believe that you have . . . fixed your interest on me."

He raised an eyebrow. "Take a look at those dragons over there. See the one with the purple turban and the four ostrich feathers?"

She looked, and saw the wagging fans and sidelong glances. Perhaps he was right. And if the Duchess of Oldenburgh talked about the bed . . . "But they are looking at Dezzie too."

"So they are. Hmm."

Her mind raced. Some way. There must be some way out of this.

"I'll wager that by tomorrow—"

"That's it!"

He almost missed a step. "That's what?"

"Can you say it was a wager? That you dared him to do it?"

He considered this for a moment. "It just might work." His smile warmed her. "I congratulate you, Miss Dudley. You have a felicitous turn of mind."

She shrugged. "*Devious* is perhaps a better word. But when one is Mama's child, one learns to be inventive."

He nodded. "I can well believe that."

The dance was soon finished, and he led her back to the sidelines. "Now," he said, "you must laugh and smile."

She tried but it was not easy, since what she most wished to do was run away and hide. First the Celestial Bed and now this. Would the embarrassments never stop?

His eyes gleamed. "A little more glee, please. We have indulged ourselves in a caper and must look like we're enjoying it. I'm going to find that pea-brained nephew of mine. You seek out Dezzie immediately and tell her what has transpired.

Do you think she can carry it off?"

"I don't know. But I'm sure she'll try."

She found Dezzie almost immediately and drew her aside. It took only a few moments to tell her what had been decided on and to instruct her about what to do.

"Yes, of course," she said. "I shall do it for my Lockwood. I shall not waver."

Licia sighed. Dezzie was still a scatterbrain. But she was obviously in love. Now they had only to stand up under attack.

❋ 6 ❋

The attack did not come until the next morning. Licia had lain awake long into the night, her mind busy with the events of the evening, reliving time after time the pleasure of those dances with the duke.

And Dezzie had tossed and turned, filling the night with endless, unanswerable questions.

But now, with breakfast behind them, they faced Mama and Aunt Hortense in the library. "Wager or not, that was a stupid thing to do," Aunt Hortense said. "The Countess Lieven and all the others . . . they will be simply scandalized by this."

"And why," interjected Mama, "did you have to break the rules with *that boy?*"

She fixed an accusing eye on Licia. "And you! What were you doing spending so much time with the duke? You know Dezzie means to marry him."

"Mama, I don't!"

Mama shifted her gaze to Dezzie again. "Quiet! I'm the one to say whom you'll marry."

Dezzie subsided with a sniffle. If only she didn't lose her resolve, Licia thought.

Then help came from another direction. Penelope said, "Perhaps Dezzie lost count, Aunt Dorothea. When one has danced every dance, all night long, how can one be expected to remember?"

Mama's face brightened at this reminder of Dezzie's triumph. But Dezzie almost spoiled it by crying, "Oh, I re—"

She stopped, warned by Penelope's sudden cough. "Cousin Penelope is right, Mama. It was a marvelous evening. Thank you, Mama. Thank you so much."

Mama's expression remained softened for a moment, but then it grew stern again. "It will all be to no avail if you insist on behaving so poorly." She frowned. "The next time the duke comes to call, you must make it up to him." She turned to Licia. "And you . . . you must refuse to see him."

Licia felt as though the whole room had suddenly been tilted sideways. She took a deep breath and steadied herself. "Mama, the duke is Penelope's friend. I cannot be rude to him. It's true, the wager was wrong. But it was meant as a jest. I cannot refuse to see him, unless Aunt Hortense means to bar him from the house."

Mama stamped her foot. "She can't do that, you ridiculous girl. Dezzie has to be able to see him."

"Then so must I. To do otherwise would be very rude."

Mama stamped her foot again, so hard that the delicate Sèvres porcelain on the mantelpiece quivered. "You are making me extremely angry."

"Really, Aunt Dorothea," Penelope intervened. "Licia had made a good point. Ravenworth has been most kind to your whole family. It would be very unseemly to treat him as you suggest. Scandalous, in fact."

Mama digested this in fuming silence for several moments. "Well, since I mean for him to marry Dezzie, I suppose Licia will have to be civil to him. But I still don't understand why she allowed him to waste his time talking to her when he should have been with Dezzie. She might have known better."

It wasn't a waste to me! Licia wanted to scream. *It was the most wonderful evening of my life!* But of course she remained silent.

It was Aunt Hortense who spoke. "Dorothea, stop spouting such nonsense! Ravenworth is not a little boy to be ordered about. He will spend his evenings in the way he wishes." She chuckled. "And not you or I or anyone else is ever going to convince him otherwise."

Dezzie sniffled again, and Licia sent her a warning glance. Dezzie must learn not to openly oppose Mama. It was a useless undertaking. But evidently Dezzie could bear no more. "Mama, please, you must listen to me."

"I have heard all I wish to hear," Mama said sternly.

But Dezzie was not to be stopped. "You *must* listen. I shall never marry Ravenworth. He has said he wishes never to marry."

"You will change his mind," Mama said with that awful complacency that allowed for no will but her own.

"Mama! I do not love him. And he is all wrong for me."

Dezzie had been goaded past endurance or she would never have stood up to Mama in this startling fashion.

"Love has nothing to do with it," Mama cried. "I say you shall marry the duke. And you shall."

"No, I shan't!" Dezzie wailed. "I cannot marry him. I love someone else!"

Mama's face grew an alarming red. "You impertinent girl! How dare you speak to me like that? Love someone else, indeed! I suppose you think you love that boy, that Lockford!"

"Lockwood, Mama. Lockwood. And I do love him. I shall always love him. Oh, how can you be so cruel?" And she burst into tears and rushed from the room.

Licia swallowed over the lump Dezzie's speech had raised in her throat. Dezzie had been foolhardy to face her mother like that. It was better to fight her unobtrusively, as Penelope did her mama. Still, Dezzie had done a very brave thing.

"Really, Dorothea, you must give it up," Aunt Hortense was saying. "Obviously the child has no feeling for Ravenworth."

"It will develop," said Mama stubbornly.

"As yours developed for Mr. Dudley?" inquired Penelope far too sweetly.

Mama's frown deepened. "Mr. Dudley was quite a different case. I was much more mature than—"

Aunt Hortense snorted and was not quite successful at turning it into a cough.

"I have heard enough," said Mama, leaping to her feet. "Dezzie will wed the duke." And she marched from the room in a dudgeon.

Aunt Hortense cast Licia a sympathetic smile. "I'd forgotten how difficult your mama is to deal with. Still, this escapade does trouble me. Dezzie might, as Penelope suggested, have simply not remembered how many dances she had with young Lockwood. But you, I'm sure, were aware of what you were about. And certainly Ravenworth was."

Licia sighed. Aunt Hortense was a sensible person. It seemed wisest to confide in her. "You're quite right, Aunt. When Ravenworth saw what his nephew was doing, he suggested that we do the same. It was his hope that the gossips would fix on us. I did not think that so possible since I am hardly in the marriage line." She had to swallow before she could continue. "And then we hit on the idea of the wager. It takes the onus off us ladies and makes it all seem some prank of the gentlemen's devising."

"Very intelligent." Aunt Hortense smiled. "And whose idea was that?"

Licia felt herself flushing. "I believe it was mine, Aunt."

"Very good."

"Aunt, you will not tell Mama?"

"Of course not. And you will continue to converse with Ravenworth. It's apparent that he enjoys your company."

"Thank you, Aunt." The thought made her feel warm inside. If Aunt Hortense believed it true, it must be so. "I suppose it is only that London ladies are not well equipped to discuss the things that interest him."

"Perhaps," said Aunt Hortense thoughtfully. "At any rate, he is always a welcome guest here. No matter what your mama says."

"And will you continue to receive Lockwood?" Licia asked. "I'm afraid that when Mama thinks of it, she will try to have him turned away."

"I will not turn him away," Aunt Hortense promised. "Eglantine would not like it. Besides, it's plain to see that the girl's in love."

"Do you think, Mama, that it's wise to marry for love?" Penelope's question was asked in the most casual of tones. But that did not deceive Licia.

"Of course," said Aunt Hortense. "Providing other things are all in order."

"Other things?" inquired Licia, watching Penelope's face.

"Yes," Aunt Hortense continued. "After all, it isn't as though the girl wanted to marry a tradesman or some foreigner. She's staying within the ton."

Penelope's complexion turned pale and Licia swallowed a sigh. Her cousin was not going to have an easy time of it. That much was certain.

Sometime later Penelope and Licia went upstairs to find Dezzie. She was lying on the bed, her face swollen and wet with tears. "Oh, Licia. I am so miserable! Whatever shall I do?"

"The first thing," said Penelope sternly, "is to stop that sniveling."

"But Mama is going to make me marry Ravenworth!"

"Nonsense! First off, your mama cannot *make* you marry anyone. And second, David has no desire to marry you. Listen . . ." She perched on the edge of the great bed. "There's no need for these hysterics. Your mama is not nearly so fierce as mine."

Dezzie stopped sniffling and sat up. "That's true. But how did you—"

"We simply refused. And we kept on refusing. And finally Mama tired of insisting."

Dezzie sighed. "I shall never give in. But Mama is so determined. And how long will Lockwood wait? Oh, if only the duke would fix his interest somewhere else!"

Penelope looked thoughtful. "That is not such a bad idea."

"But, but . . ." Licia's stomach had taken a sudden tumbling fit. "He doesn't wish to marry."

"He could pretend!" Dezzie cried. "He could find some lady and pretend till Mama gives up and lets me wed my Lockwood." She reached for Licia's hands. "Oh, dear Licia, I know I have not been the best sister, but would you do this for me? Would you ask the duke to fix his interest on someone?"

The room had taken on an alarming tendency to sway. "I? How can I ask such a thing? Penelope is the one to do it."

Penelope shook her head. "No, I think Licia should do it."

"But how . . ." How could she ask Ravenworth to fix his attention on some other woman when she wanted him to . . . no, she could not allow herself to think like that. It would lead to no good conclusion.

"Please, Licia." Dezzie's eyes brimmed with tears. "I know you think I'm a foolish green girl, but . . ."

Automatically Licia patted her sister's hand. "No, dear. I don't think that."

"But I do love Lockwood. And if Mama prevents our marrying, I shall never wed another." She cast her eyes heavenward. "As I live and breathe, I swear it."

Licia looked to her cousin for help, but Penelope was nodding. "Listen to Dezzie," she said. "In this matter of love she is right. When you love someone, really love someone, you love them forever."

Dezzie turned and clasped her cousin in a fervent embrace. "Oh, thank you, dear Penelope. How lovely of you to understand."

"Yes, I do understand." Penelope looked to Licia. "So how shall you broach the subject to Ravenworth?"

With the two of them gazing at her like that she knew she had no chance of weaseling out. "I have not the slightest idea. I shall have to wait till the time comes."

"Oh, dear!" Dezzie wailed.

"Now what is wrong?"

"Lockwood. He's coming to call today. I did not have a chance to warn him. The duke spirited him away immediately. He will come and Mama will turn him away. And I shall never see his face again!" And she burst into fresh sobs.

Licia, whose own inclination was to join her sister in wailing, could find no comforting words to utter. She was feeling so desolate herself that it took all her effort to keep a calm expression.

It was Penelope who administered the comforting words, Penelope who said, "Don't be such a goose. No matter what your mama wants, Mama will never turn Lockwood away. He is the duchess's grandson after all. And Mama and the duchess have been bosom bows since childhood."

Dezzie wiped at her eyes. "But what about this awful thing

we did—dancing three times like that? Do you think the ton will forgive us?"

"It was not a wise thing to do," said Penelope, "but I think the wager will carry it off." She smiled at Licia. "That was a most inventive idea, Cousin."

Licia shrugged and pressed a hand to her throbbing temple. "There was so little time. It was all I could think of."

"Poor Licia," said Dezzie, full of concern. "Do you have the headache? Come, lie upon the bed and let me bring you a cold cloth."

Though no amount of cold cloths would relieve the ache she felt at the thought of Ravenworth showing attention to another woman, Licia sighed and acquiesced. For once in her life she lay down and let her sister do the ministering.

Licia lay in the darkened room for about an hour. Then, unable to bear the inactivity and the consequent rioting of her thoughts, she rose, pronounced herself fit again, and went downstairs with the others.

Once Mama had declared an intention, she fully expected it to be carried out. And since no one bothered to disagree with her over the future she so rosily painted, she prattled on in great glee.

But when she got to elaborating on the furnishings of the castle Ravenworth was going to purchase for Dezzie, Licia felt the headache returning in full force. She was about to say so when Herberts announced, "The Duke of Ravenworth. Viscount Lockwood."

Mama's expression went from pleasure to displeasure so swiftly, it was almost amusing.

But Aunt Hortense did not wait for her to speak. "A few moments, Herberts. Then show them in."

As Herberts left, she turned to her sister. "Now,

Dorothea, if you cannot behave yourself, you may leave the room. Ravenworth is the son of my dearest friend and I will not have him or their relations slighted."

Mama looked pouty. But she said, "Very well. If you must put your friends above *your* relations."

"Dorothea!"

But there was time for no more words. The duke and the viscount entered. Lockwood's eyes went immediately to Dezzie, and Mama frowned fiercely.

"Good day, David," said Penelope. "I see you are looking in good shape this afternoon."

Ravenworth nodded. "Of course, Cousin. We have come to see how you ladies are faring." His eyes met Licia's and sent her a message of reassurance. But he could not know that the task that faced her now was far more frightening than anything Mama might say to her.

They made small talk for a few minutes, and then Penelope said, "I believe some fresh air would do us good. Shall we take a turn in the garden?"

Mama looked about to protest. But it was only a small courtyard garden. And Dezzie and the duke would be out there together, so she remained silent.

Ravenworth did not speak to Licia till they had reached the little garden. The late April sun was warm on her face, but her heart was cold. For up there in the quiet of her bedchamber she had come to a chilling realization.

"Well, now," said Penelope with false cheerfulness, "I shall just take the youngsters over there to admire the daffodils." And herding them before her, she left Licia to her fate.

Ravenworth turned to her immediately. "Penelope is acting strangely again. What is wrong?"

Licia twisted her handkerchief in nervous fingers. How was she to say this? "Nothing is wrong. At least, not exactly."

The duke sighed. "Then why did Penelope leave us alone in this obvious fashion?"

There was no help for it. She would have to press on. Dezzie's future lay in her hands. "Mama . . . Dezzie . . . that is . . . we need your help."

He took one of her trembling hands in his own. "You know I should be glad to help you in any way I can."

"Yes, yes. I know." She withdrew her fingers. How could she think with her hand in his? "As you suggested last evening, Dezzie has a decided *tendre* for your nephew."

He nodded. "Yes, and he has fixed his interest on her. Nothing amiss there."

She sighed. "I'm afraid there is. Mama will not allow Lockwood's courtship."

"Because she wants your sister to land a bigger fish?"

"Yes, in fact"—it had to be said—"she wants her to land you."

Apparently the thought had not previously occurred to him. His expression was one of stunned amazement. "Me?"

"Yes, Your Grace. And as long as you are—available—Mama will not allow Dezzie another suitor."

"But I have no interest in marriage. I have said so repeatedly."

"Mama hears only what fits her plans. She expects Dezzie to snare you."

His frown was frightening. "That woman! Well, she'll just be disappointed. It will never happen."

Licia nodded. "Of course. But Mama is so difficult to dissuade, and Dezzie is much afraid of losing your nephew."

"What a bumble broth. And all because your Mama cannot be made to listen to reason."

She had no desire to defend Mama. "I know. But Dezzie has come up with a plan."

"Dezzie!"

"Yes, I know. She is scatterbrained. But it is a good plan."

His sigh was deep and heartfelt. "So I collect I must hear it."

"Dezzie thinks—and so do I—that if you were to fix your interest on some other young woman, escort her about, and appear to court her, Mama might be brought to accept the truth." There, she had said it, and she did not feel in the least better.

His eyebrow rose. "I see. But this admirable plan has one fatal flaw."

"It has?" She could not think what it could be, but she was glad to hear of it.

"Indeed. As you know, I don't hold with the institution of marriage. If I fix my interest on some young woman, she should ultimately be disappointed. Don't you think it cruel to raise her hopes and then dash them?"

She saw a glimmer of light. If he would not do it, she might still have his company. "I . . . I had not considered that."

"I've no desire to have some outraged mama after me." He frowned thoughtfully. "However, the plan does have merit."

"It does?"

"Yes. And I believe I see a way to put it into action."

Her heart fell again. She was going to lose him. "What is it?"

"There is one young woman who could fill the part. And she would not be hurt because she would be in on the secret from the start."

Her mind was a confused whirl. Who was this woman he could trust so? "P-Penelope?" she stammered.

"Oh, no. That would never wash." He regarded her soberly. "I am thinking of you."

"Me!" She sank down on a nearby bench, joy and fear mingling in her breast in a whirlwind of confusion.

He settled beside her. "Of course, it would mean much turbulence from your mama. But I believe we could convince her."

"We might. She . . . she has already chastised me for wasting your time."

He frowned. "Wasting?"

"Yes, because I talked with you when she wished you to be occupied with Dezzie."

He frowned fiercely. "She will have to learn. So, are you willing?"

"I am willing. But, Your Grace, I am not young and beautiful. Will the ton believe . . ."

He smiled at her in a way that quite weakened her knees. "They will believe," he promised. "I shall dance constant attendance on you. Act besotted with love. Practically live in your pocket." He paused. "But you—can you convince the world of your affection for me?"

Thank God he need never know her pretense would be no pretense at all. "I have never been good at lying, Your Grace. But I shall certainly try. For Dezzie's sake."

"Good." He took her hand once more in his. "Then the bargain is sealed."

He got to his feet and pulled her up. "Come, my dear. First we'll instruct the others in their parts. Then we'll return to the house and commence our campaign."

And Licia, hardly knowing whether to laugh or cry, allowed him to lead her to the others.

 7

Mama and Hortense were sipping tea. Mama stared rather pointedly over her teacup as the group seated itself. Then she fastened her falsely charming smile on the duke. "Your Grace, last night the Duchess of Oldenburgh—such a charming woman—she was telling me about this actor. Mr. Kemble is his name. It seems he does Hamlet. And she says he's most enjoyable to watch. Have you seen him?"

Ravenworth didn't even raise an eyebrow, though by now he must be quite conversant with Mama's tricks. "Yes, of course, Mrs. Dudley. All London knows of him. I myself prefer Kean, the new man at Drury Lane. But Kemble is very good at what he does."

Mama sighed. "My poor Dezzie has been so long denied these fine performances. If only she had some nice gentleman to escort her to the theater."

"I—" Lockwood stopped and rubbed the arm the duke had surreptitiously pinched. "That is, Mr. Kemble is very good. He has much dignity of expression."

For all the attention Mama paid him, the viscount might as well have remained silent. "Yes." Mama sighed again. "I am sure Dezzie would like to see this wondrous play."

Licia swallowed a sigh of her own. How could Mama be so obvious? In spite of all the duke knew about her, it was acutely embarrassing.

And then Ravenworth's eyes met hers—and they were twinkling. He was actually enjoying this!

Mama beamed and Aunt Hortense frowned, but Licia just sat there, thinking. He would probably begin his campaign at the play. How long would it take them to convince Mama that her plans were useless? Probably a long time.

The rush of pleasure this thought brought her was quite disconcerting. No matter how long Ravenworth paid court to her, the end result would be the same. Dezzie would have the viscount. And her sister would have no one.

Still, she'd never been one to snivel, and she would not begin now. If all she was to have was this pretend courtship, she would enjoy every precious second of it.

"As soon as possible," Mama was saying. "I am dying to see this divine man."

"Shall we say Friday next?" Ravenworth inquired. "I believe that will be his next performance of the melancholy Dane."

When Mama nodded, he got to his feet. "Come, Lockwood, we must be off. We've things to attend to."

The viscount rose dutifully and bent to kiss Dezzie's hand. Then, to Licia's surprise, Ravenworth bent to hers. The touch of his lips on her fingers sent little whispers of delight shivering over her. And when he looked into her eyes and smiled, she thought her heart would melt and run right out her fingertips.

"I shall be seeing you soon," he said. And there was such promise in his voice that she was hard put to remember that this was all acting on his part.

She knew she was blushing as she replied, "I shall look forward to it, Your Grace." She watched him leave, and her heart beat more rapidly. In his bottle-green coat and fawn inexpressibles he was surely the most magnificent man in London.

The door had barely closed behind him when Dorothea

erupted. "Delicia Marie Dudley! Wipe that ridiculous smirk off your face! You are not going anywhere. When the duke arrives to take us to the theater, you will be ill."

"Dorothea!" Plainly Aunt Hortense could contain herself no longer. "It is you who is being ridiculous."

Mama bristled but Aunt Hortense hurried on. "Licia is not going to sit at home alone just because you have some addlepated notion in your head."

Mama pouted. "She's an ungrateful daughter. And I'm most unhappy with her."

Licia heard the hard words, but they did not penetrate her heart. At that moment nothing could hurt her. She was still basking in the glow of Ravenworth's smile.

"Aunt Dorothea, what bits of London gossip did you overhear last night?" Penelope was obviously trying to introduce a less sensitive subject. And she proved successful.

Mama's pout disappeared. "The dear duchess—you know, she stayed by me all evening, and she said the most glowing things concerning Dezzie's come-out. Well, she had heard about this lady. I cannot recall her name. At any rate, this lady had taken up with one of those artist fellows. A sculptor, I think."

Licia's eyes went to Penelope. Her cousin had paled and was now staring resolutely at the wall, her hands rigid in her lap. Pray God she wouldn't say something and give herself away.

Aunt Hortense straightened. "My word, some women have no sense of social consequence. An artist, you say. Why, an artist is lower than . . . than a Frenchman!"

Licia saw that Penelope was struggling with herself. If she spoke now, she might well give the whole thing away.

And so she herself spoke. "Dear aunt, I'm afraid I don't understand."

"Understand what?"

"I thought you were most appreciative of Mr. Turner's paintings."

Aunt Hortense looked surprised. "I am, child. The man does such wonders. He's a veritable genius."

"Then why is an artistic person not fit company for a lady?"

Aunt Hortense smiled patiently. "My dear, talent and class do not necessarily go hand in hand. A lady must marry within her class." She cast a glance at Mama whose pout showed signs of returning. "Or above it."

"So a lady cannot marry a man of genius even though she might love him?"

Aunt Hortense's smile was becoming strained. "Of course she cannot. Her family would disown her."

"But, Aunt, what if he were an upright, honorable man?"

"That doesn't signify." Aunt Hortense was now frowning. "I hope that you or Dezzie are not considering such a scandalous thing."

Here, at least, Licia could be truthful. "Of course not, Aunt. Neither of us have any such inclination."

"Good. I should hope not. Penelope, where are you going?"

Penelope paused in the doorway. "I find that I am still fatigued from last night, Mama. It was such a brilliant party. So I thought I might lie down for a while before dinner."

Licia got to her feet. "I, too, have some things to attend to in my room. If you'll excuse me . . ."

Aunt Hortense nodded. "Run along. Don't know what's wrong with young people these days. No stamina. Why, in my time . . ."

"Thank you," said Penelope when they had reached the safety of her room. "I thought I should explode! Harry is such a wonderful man. And just because he is a commoner, our love is doomed. Oh, Licia, what shall I do?"

Licia shook her head. "I simply do not know. Aunt Hortense seems quite firm." She sighed. "I believe I understand you when you speak about being happy anywhere with him. But there is something to what your mama says too. You must have shelter—food and clothing."

Penelope's laughter held no amusement. "Look at me, Licia. I am a plain woman. Not ugly, perhaps, but plain. And I do not care. I do not need—or even want—fine gowns and furnishings. Why, I wager that Harry and I could live comfortably for an entire year on the cost of that one atrocious gown. All I need is Harry's love."

She drew herself up. "Since it appears that Mama will never give in, I shall have to prevail on Harry. I do not intend to give him up." She pressed a hand to her temple. "But now I am afraid I do have the headache. And I am supposed to see him this afternoon."

"Do you think perhaps you go too often to the gallery?"

"Perhaps. I don't know. But I cannot go like this." She sank down on the chaise. "He will see my distress and it will pain him."

She clasped Licia's hand. "Could you carry a note to Harry for me?"

"I? Go to the gallery? But how shall I get away? And what about Dezzie? If I go out, she will want to come along. And you know she can't keep a secret."

Penelope groaned. "Oh, this headache is abominable. I really cannot think. Please, Cousin, I know you can manage it. Just get my note to him."

Licia sighed. She did not want to go out. Even less did she want to be the bearer of clandestine notes. If Aunt Hortense discovered her doing such a thing, she might well take

Mama's part and exile such an ungrateful young woman from their theater excursion.

But Penelope was looking at her with pleading eyes. And how should she feel if Ravenworth really loved her and she were in a similar situation? There was no doubt in her mind that if the roles were reversed, Penelope would undertake such a mission. And so she surrendered to the inevitable. "Very well."

"Oh, thank you." Penelope rose and hurried to her rose-wood desk. "It will be a short note."

A short time later Licia descended the great stairs. The note was safely tucked away in her reticule, but she was not yet sure what she would say.

Aunt Hortense had lingered over tea and fortunately was still alone. "Well, my dear, did you finish attending to things?"

"Yes, Aunt. Do you suppose I might have the carriage for a little while?" She forced herself to smile apologetically. "I find last night's entertainment leaves me restless. I should like to ride about a little. Perhaps look again at a painting at the gallery. There was one there I am much taken with."

"I suppose it is all right. Is your sister going?"

Licia lowered her voice. "I have not asked her. I know it sounds dreadful, Aunt. But sometimes she talks so much, I cannot think. And I must always be looking out for her."

Aunt Hortense smiled. "I quite understand, my dear. I used to feel the same about your mama." She winked. "Go down the back way. Tell Ben Dibbens I sent you. And I will say you have gone on an errand for me."

Licia bent and kissed her aunt's white cheek. "Thank you, you are—"

"Scat. Hurry now."

Scurrying out through the kitchen, Licia blinked back the tears. In most ways Aunt Hortense was most understanding, most kind. But how angry she would be if she discovered this ruse.

Of course, she reminded herself, everything she had said had been quite true. It was the things she had left unsaid that were so dreadful. And so damning if she were discovered.

The carriage stopped in front of Turner's gallery long before Licia was ready for it. She had not seen a thing in the teeming streets through which they'd passed. Her mind had been a whirl of catastrophic events. What if the gallery were full of people? What if no opportunity to pass the note arose? What if . . .

"Turner's Gallery, miss." Dibbens obviously expected her to get down.

And so she had no recourse but to go inside. She would hurry, she told herself. Get this dreadful task finished with.

So when she saw Harry Bates approaching her, she felt more than a little relief.

"Miss Dudley," he said, "I did not expect to see you today."

"I—I find myself restless after last night's festivities. And I thought a little drive might calm me." She glanced around. There were others within earshot. And they might see. She should have folded the message small and kept it in her palm. She could not reach in her reticule for it with all these people about.

"Also, there was a painting I liked very much. I am thinking . . ." The words came hard. She was not accustomed to lying. "I am thinking of buying it as a gift."

"I understand," said Harry. "You want another look at it. Which painting was it?"

"*Frosty . . . Frosty Morning.*"

"Of course. It's over this way. But I must tell you. Someone else has already spoken for it."

"Who?" She asked the question quite without thinking, and she really didn't care about the answer. But she was surprised when he frowned and said, "I'm sorry. I am not at liberty to say. Some of our patrons wish to remain anonymous."

"I see." She pushed the mysterious purchaser from her mind. "Well, I shall just have another look at it before it's gone." She hesitated. "Perhaps when you have finished your business with the others you will return. And . . . and show me something along the same line?"

"I shall be glad to, miss."

After he left her, she opened her reticule. Fortunately the note was on the small side. She maneuvered it into her palm and covered it with a handkerchief before she withdrew her hand. There, no one should notice it now.

It seemed a long time before Harry Bates returned. And unfortunately the glories of *Frosty Morning* were completely lost on her. She wanted only to finish this dreadful task and be on her way.

"So," he said, "perhaps you would like to see—"

"No thank you." The strain was too much. "I find I must go. Perhaps another time." And she extended her hand, the note hidden in her palm.

He had evidently been expecting as much. His face showed no expression of surprise, and when their hands parted, the note remained in his. Surreptitiously he transferred it to his pocket. "Good day, Miss Dudley."

She drew a deep breath as he left her. At least the deed was done. How did spies do this sort of thing all the time? It was dreadfully hard on the nerves.

"Admiring the frost?" said a voice by her elbow.

"Ravenworth!" Her heart rose up in her throat. "What are you doing here?"

"I might ask you the same."

She repeated the lie yet again. "I was restless and wished to see the paintings."

"And is that all?"

Her heart threatened to jump right out of her mouth. But she managed to say "All?"

"Yes, all."

He looked so stern, almost ferocious. Could he have seen? "I do not understand."

"Very well, I shall explain. I believe that earlier today we devised a plan."

She nodded.

"It is a plan fraught with difficulties. Would you not agree?"

"Yes, Your Grace."

"And I undertake it at no little risk to my reputation."

"Your reputation?"

"Yes, my reputation. Here I am about to forsake my role as Corinthian and undertake that of lovesick Lothario. And I find the object of my affections tête-à-tête with another man."

"Your Grace! We were discussing pictures."

"Indeed." He looked around, then lowered his voice. "Really, Miss Dudley. It is not *de rigueur* to pass notes to men in public places. How are we to convince your mama of our undying passion if word of this gets about?"

"Your Grace, I should never knowingly put our plan in jeopardy. Surely you must realize that. The note was merely . . ." The thought came to her out of nowhere, and she grabbed it with relief. "It was a few lines of instruction from Penelope concerning the painting she wishes to purchase."

His frown lightened a little. "Why did she not come herself?"

"She has a headache. And I was restless. So she entrusted the errand to me. Truly, Your Grace. I am very grateful to you for your help. And I should certainly not wish to do anything that would make things more difficult."

Slowly his frown vanished. "Perhaps I should beg your pardon," he said finally. "I find I make quite a jealous swain."

If only, she thought, such jealousy were real. But it was his reputation he was thinking of, not her. "It was my fault, Your Grace. I was nervous about delivering the message, and I bungled it."

His smile wrapped her in the most delicious warmth. "Do not turn around," he said, all the while continuing to smile. "But smile at me."

There was little need for that instruction. His smile had already elicited one from her. But he had piqued her curiosity. "What is it? Why can't I turn?"

"Across the room. The Countess Lieven. And she has been observing us. I think, my dear, that we are well on our way to becoming an item. We have just had our first lovers' quarrel. And in public. The whole ton will know of it by nightfall."

He pulled her arm through his. "Smile some more while we stroll and complete the effect."

8

And so the days came and went. Every afternoon Ravenworth arrived, usually with his nephew in tow. True to his word, the duke danced attendance on Licia like the most devoted of suitors. But Mama, secure in her own little world, beamed happily, content that all his intentions were for Dezzie. And no one cared to try to disabuse her of this absurd notion. At least not yet.

The day of their theater excursion finally arrived. In the afternoon Mama began dropping not so subtle hints. "Licia, my dear, you are looking positively haggard. Are you sure you're not ill?"

But Licia would not be pressured. "Mama, I am feeling fine. I wouldn't miss Mr. Kemble's performance for anything."

Coming down the stairs in her gown of lavender silk with bishop sleeves and a softly draped skirt, Licia swallowed a sigh. If only mama wasn't accompanying them. How marvelous it would be to attend the theater alone with Ravenworth, to be able to discuss the play without Mama's interruptions. But of course that would never happen.

In the carriage Ravenworth contrived to get Penelope on one side of him and Licia on the other. He gave her a reassuring smile, but she found it difficult to smile in return. To the best of her knowledge their arrangement had accomplished one thing, and one thing only. It had made clear to her the inescapable fact that she had let herself develop a feeling for the duke.

It was a pea-brained thing to do. And she certainly hadn't meant to allow it. But emotions did not wait on permission. And the uncomfortable truth was that every moment she spent in his company increased the intensity of her feelings for him.

She must never lose sight of the fact—she could not allow herself to do so—that this was all make-believe. The light in his eyes, the smile on his lips, the pressure of his fingers—all were trappings to make their performance more convincing.

She looked across to the other seat, where Dezzie sat between Mama and Aunt Hortense. Dezzie was clearly disappointed that Lockwood was not one of the party. Her pretty lips were pursed in a pout that looked very much like one of Mama's. But there was nothing Licia could do about it at the moment.

When they arrived at Covent Garden, the street was congested to the extreme. Coachman battled coachman with verbal insults that would have reddened the ears of any lady who allowed herself to overhear them. The crush was terrible, and there was no chance for conversation in such a hubbub. But Ravenworth managed quite well, leading them all to safety through the throng.

Climbing to their box, Dezzie exclaimed. "Oh, isn't this the most marvelous place?" But Licia, though she looked, could register little. All her senses were intent on the man to whose arm she clung.

When they reached the box, Mama's mouth took on a mutinous pout. Licia's heart began to sink. Mama meant to get between them, to keep Ravenworth from her older daughter's side.

But the duke was before her. He put Mama and Aunt Hortense and Dezzie in the front row. Then he seated himself between Penelope and Licia in the back. He smiled at

Penelope. "I much prefer this gown to that sausage casing you insisted on wearing the other night."

Penelope smiled. "So do I."

Licia nodded in agreement. This tunic dress of soft gray silk, though it could not make her beautiful, made Penelope look quite nice. It gave her a quiet dignity.

"What are you whispering about back there?" demanded Mama crossly.

"The duke is complimenting me on my gown," Penelope replied with a look at the others.

"Oh. Well, I'm sure I don't see why he put Dezzie up here with us. She belongs with you young people." Such a look of amusement passed between Penelope and Ravenworth that Licia had to bite her lip not to laugh.

"You're quite right, Aunt," said Penelope. "I suppose Ravenworth thought Dezzie could see better up there. But if she wants to change places with me. I shall be glad to do so."

"Dezzie, change places with your cousin."

"But, Mama, I want to see—"

"Now."

Dezzie got to her feet, her lower lip trembling, and changed seats with Penelope. But while Mama was saying complacently, "There, that's much better," Ravenworth was leaning forward and whispering something in Dezzie's ear. She brightened immediately and settled into her seat with a happy smile.

"Now, that that is settled," the duke said to Licia, "let me help you with this mantle." The touch of his fingers on the nape of her neck sent her into a fit of trembling. Oh, why had she been so foolish? Why hadn't she seen this coming?

"May I say," he went on in a tone calculated to reach Mama's ears, "that you are looking lovely tonight? That lavender certainly becomes you."

Since Dezzie's gown was blue, there was no way Mama could ignore that this compliment was meant for Licia. But mama was never one to be thwarted. "Don't you think Dezzie's gown is lovely, Your Grace? She has such a sense of fashion."

Since Dezzie's gown was one of those Licia had come to think of as sausage gowns, she had to smile.

Ravenworth smiled, too, and pressed her fingers. "Miss Desiree must get her fashion sense from her mama."

This observation sent Aunt Hortense into a fit of coughing. She might not know much about fashion, but she was quick enough at recognizing the duke's dry humor.

"Please, Your Grace," said Dezzie, "name for me some of these people."

Obligingly Ravenworth pointed out "Golden" Ball, Lord Alvanley, "King" Allen, and other well-known figures. "Over there, the tall dark woman in the rubies. That is the Countess Lieven. One of the patronesses of Almack's."

"Oh." Dezzie's eyes widened. "Do you think we shall be invited there?"

The duke shrugged. "Perhaps. But the place is greatly overrated. The cake is stale and the lemonade warm." He turned to Licia. "The company is not of the best, either." He gave her a smile that turned her bones to water.

"Why do . . ." she began.

The door to the box opened and Lockwood entered. "I say, Ravenworth, got an extra place here? I gave my box to Mama for tonight and she's filled it to overflowing. No place in there for another soul, not even the living skeleton from the raree-show."

Ravenworth chuckled. "You're welcome here," he said. "Come in and take a seat."

Licia could see Mama's back stiffening. But Penelope and

Ravenworth had outfoxed her. They had deliberately set up the situation so that *she* would move Dezzie to the back. Most women would have conceded defeat, but not Mama. As always, she only accepted what fit her plans.

"Dezzie, dear, I do wish you were up here by me. You can see so much."

"I can see quite well, Mama."

"Yes, perhaps. But . . ."

Dezzie cast the duke a look of appeal. "Now that Miss Desiree is back here," he said, "I think it wise for her to stay. I may wish to comment on the finer points of the play." His eyes twinkled at Licia, but his tone remained pompous. "I do think it important that a young woman have a proper appreciation of the theater."

"Yes, yes, of course," replied Mama. "Whatever you think best, Your Grace."

And then, most fortunately, the curtain rose. The story of poor Hamlet was not unfamiliar to her, and Licia watched with great interest. Somehow, though, when intermission came, she was aware of a sense of disappointment. "It seems so . . ."

"Unreal?" Ravenworth suggested.

"Yes, how did you know?"

"You're not the only one to say it. Kemble is a follower of the old school, the school of Art. Every nuance, every gesture, is built on convention. So Art becomes an accretion of many performances."

"He has great dignity," Licia replied. "But somehow he does not seem to fit the part."

The duke smiled. "Critics speak of his tragic cast and stately dignity, but they also point out his affectations. Like that Order of the Elephant that he wears, an order that did not exist in Hamlet's lifetime."

"He does have great skill in declamation," Licia said. "Perhaps he is best in parts that call for Roman greatness and tragic eloquence, rather than the kind of vacillation that marks poor Hamlet's state of mind."

"You have a quick intelligence, my dear."

His fingers closed over hers, and for a second she could think of nothing but their warmth and the sound of his voice saying, "My dear."

"One day soon I'll take you to see Kean. Remember? I mentioned him the other day."

She nodded. "And does he play Hamlet differently?"

"Oh, yes. Kean is a proponent of the school of Nature. He claims every performer may put his own stamp upon the role. And to do so he draws from nature. His Hamlet is altogether different. More melancholy, more—"

Mama half turned in her chair. "I do not see how anyone can be compared to Mr. Kemble. The man is divine. An Olympian. Such a fine figure. And the resonances of his voice . . . why, he sends chills down my spine."

Dezzie and Lockwood, murmuring to each other in the corner, hadn't heard a word of this. But when Mama said, "Dezzie, listen carefully to the duke," her sister replied, "Yes, Mama, of course."

After Hamlet had been dispatched to the other world with suitable dignity and the afterpiece had made them all laugh, they got to their feet. "Thank you for an enjoyable evening," Aunt Hortense said to the duke. "I always enjoy the theater."

"Oh, but we cannot leave yet!" Mama cried. "We must go to the Green Room. I want to see the great man in person."

"Oh, yes," said Dezzie, obviously willing to do anything that would prolong the evening and keep Lockwood at her side.

But Licia found the idea distressing. Mama was so often

embarrassing. And who knew what she might say to the great man?

But evidently Aunt Hortense thought it wiser to give her sister her way in this. "I suppose we can go. But there will be a crush."

"That won't bother me." Mama beamed. "I just want to see him up close."

So off they went, Dezzie on Lockwood's arm and Licia on Ravenworth's. Fortunately Mama was so caught up in her enthusiasm that she failed to comment on this arrangement.

Still, Licia entered the crowded room with a sinking heart and a huge sigh. Ravenworth smiled down at her. "Such a sigh, my dear."

"It's Mama. Bringing her in here . . ."

He nodded. "I quite understand. But do not worry your pretty head about it. I shall keep her out of the suds."

In spite of her distress Licia had to laugh. She was not sure if it was because of his compliment or because he thought he could control Mama. "Your Grace," she replied, "since the day she was born my mama has been in trouble. I doubt that even you can keep her out of it."

"Perhaps not. But at least you smiled." His expression turned quizzical. "You seem so often pensive. Has our arrangement been so onerous to you?"

"Oh, no!" What did that look in his eyes mean? "I am just worried. Dezzie is so in love. And she's afraid of losing your nephew."

"Never fear." He patted the hand that rested on his arm. "I'll speak to Lockwood. Tell him I think Dezzie's the girl for him. And I do. The young pup respects my opinion, I think."

"Thank you. I shall rest easier."

"And shall you smile for me again?"

"I shall try. But—oh, dear!"

"What is it?"

"Mama! She has reached Mr. Kemble. And he does not look happy."

Mr. Kemble was a man of some stature. In his black doublet and hose he stood like some great tree while Mama fluttered before him like a foraging little bird.

Licia pulled at the duke's arm. "Please hurry, before she says something dreadful."

But it was already too late. Just as they reached Mama's side, Mr. Kemble gave her a discouraging look and said, "Please, Madame. I am an actor. My life is devoted to my art. I have no time to listen to wild tales about magical beds or the charlatans who created them."

"Well, I never!" Mama drew herself up to her full five feet and glared. "I'll have you know that Dr. Graham—"

Ravenworth slipped an arm through Mama's and expertly drew her away.

"The nerve of that man," she sputtered. "Why, Dr. Graham was a great man. He—"

"Perhaps," interrupted Ravenworth smoothly. "But, Mrs. Dudley, you have quite misunderstood the situation here."

That stopped Mama and she asked, "Misunderstood? I?"

"Quite so. Actors do not stand about in the Green Room so that they may hear the stories of people's lives."

Mama frowned in puzzlement. "But I thought it would make a good play."

Licia shuddered and the duke drew her closer.

"A good play?" He shook his head. "No, it would not. But that is beside the point. You have offended Kemble, you see. He expected words of praise about his great performance."

Mama looked almost shocked. "But I did say I liked it."

"And I'm sure he appreciated that. But that is all you

should have said." He frowned down on her. "Besides, I thought we had agreed that it was best not to mention the bed."

Mama tried to look contrite. "Yes, I suppose we did. But it is such a *good* story. And usually people are most attentive when . . ." Suddenly she noticed Licia on his other arm. "Where is Dezzie? She should be here."

"Miss Desiree and my nephew are over there. With Lady Hortense."

Mama sniffed. "I don't know why that boy keeps hanging around. Can't you send him away?"

Ravenworth stiffened. Licia could feel it in the arm she held. "I am afraid I cannot do that, Madame. I am quite too busy with my own courtship to interfere with my nephew's." And he bestowed on Licia such a dazzling smile that the whole room seemed instantly brighter.

"You are wasting your time," Mama said. "Can't you see—"

"Excuse me, Madame." Ravenworth's face had grown almost fierce. "I do not appreciate your speaking in that denigrating fashion about the woman I care for."

Mama's eyes widened. "Whatever do you mean?"

"I mean that time spent with Miss Dudley can never be considered wasted. She is a conversationalist par excellence and her company is greatly to be coveted."

Mama looked utterly amazed. "Are you talking about my Licia?"

"I am indeed."

"Well, I never!" For once Mama seemed to have no more words.

"Come," said Ravenworth. "It's time we went home."

Oh, it was. Past time, thought Licia. His defense of her had been magnificent. And to say like that, with such conviction, that she was the woman he cared for! It was hard to remember that it was all make-believe, especially when she yearned—body and soul—to have it all be true.

Lockwood took reluctant leave of Dezzie. He lingered so long over her hand that Licia feared an outburst from Mama. But evidently the duke's words had stunned her.

They rode for some moments in silence, each absorbed in thought. Then Dezzie heaved a great sigh. "Poor Ophelia. To kill herself like that for love."

Mama shook her head. "I'm sure to kill one's self is mortal sin."

"Dear Aunt Dorothea," said Penelope patiently. "We are discussing a play, not real life."

Mama sank into aggrieved silence, but Dezzie could not contain herself. "I think Ophelia did the right thing. She knew she'd lost Hamlet. If one loses a loved one, then death might be enviable."

"Desiree Dudley!" Mama's shocked expression was visible even by the carriage lights. "What a terrible thing to say!"

"I don't think it's terrible." In her own way Dezzie could be just as recalcitrant as Mama, perhaps even more so. "It's horrible to lose someone you love. It's like dying yourself."

"Perhaps," said Mama, her face setting into stubborn lines. "But I certainly should not have done such an awful thing, even when I lost Mr. Dudley."

Dezzie refused to give it up. "But you had many years with Papa. That's not like losing someone before you even get to marry them. Like Ophelia lost Hamlet. Or . . . or—"

"Juliet lost Romeo," inserted his grace helpfully.

Mama snorted. "I always did think that a silly story. If she loved him like she said, why didn't that Juliet just run off and marry him? That's what I did."

"That's right!" cried Dezzie, her eyes lighting up. "That's what you did!"

"Dorothea!" Aunt Hortense exclaimed in obvious agitation.

Mama, evidently seeing the misdirection in which she was heading, tried to set things right. "It was harder in my day. Girls actually were kept under lock and key. But enough, this is all silliness. There'll be no more talk of dying for love. Or running off."

"Yes, Mama." Dezzie sank into silence, and Mama appeared satisfied, but Licia, regarding the expression on her sister's face, knew the damage had been done, the seed planted. From this day forward Gretna Green would be in the back of Dezzie's mind. And if Mama could not be prevailed upon to grant permission, Dezzie would know exactly what to do.

The rest of the ride was made in silence. Aunt Hortense looked as though she thoroughly regretted opening her home to such a ragtag bunch. Dezzie and Penelope both sat, pensive, thinking no doubt of the men they loved and the day when they could be with them.

And Licia, with the object of her affections beside her, could think only of the time when their charade would be no more. And the weeks and months and years would stretch before her, empty of Ravenworth's companionship. She was not a person of morbid character, and she would certainly go on living. Still, she discovered a great deal of sympathy for Ophelia and for Juliet, both of whom, facing a lifetime without the men they loved, had chosen what could only seem like an easier way.

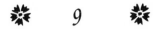 *9*

The next morning Licia went late to the breakfast table. Her appetite was not at its best. She had spent most of the night lying awake, reliving the evening's events. Most especially she had repeated to herself every golden word Ravenworth had uttered to Mama in her defense. She meant to keep them blazoned forever in her memory. How impassioned he had been. How sincere. And how good he had made her feel!

But now it was time to pay the piper. And, from the look on Mama's face, the payment was going to be high. "Licia," said Mama. Dezzie looked up from her chocolate and sent her sister a commiserating look.

Licia put down her cup and faced her parent. "Yes, Mama?"

Mama frowned. "I have spoken to you before about occupying his grace's time. You are not behaving as a proper sister should."

Dezzie began to fidget. "But, Mama—"

"Quiet," she said with a quelling look. "I am quite displeased with you too." With a sniffle, Dezzie subsided. Mama turned back to Licia. "Now, I have told you and told you that I mean for the duke to wed Dezzie. And yet you still distract him with this talk of silly things like land reform."

Licia could not let that pass. "Land reform is not silly, Mama. It was one of Papa's dearest concerns."

Mama brushed this aside. "Yes, well, that doesn't signify now. I want you to stop conversing with his grace. Give Dezzie a chance to captivate him."

Licia took a deep breath. She seldom opposed Mama outright. It was usually easier to attain her goals in a roundabout fashion. But this time that wouldn't do. "Mama, I am sorry. But I cannot do as you wish."

Mama's face began to redden. "Cannot! Well, I never! And why not, may I ask?"

"Because . . ." It took all her will to say it out loud. "Because I have formed an attachment for the duke."

Aunt Hortense's cup shivered against her saucer, and Penelope smothered a gasp.

"You have done what?" Mama demanded.

"I have formed an attachment for the duke," Licia repeated. "And I wish to marry him."

Aunt Hortense shook her head. "Upon my word! Licia a duchess!"

Mama turned on her in a fury. "Don't be such a ninny, Sister. The duke can't really be interested in Licia. Look at her! She isn't pretty at all."

Aunt Hortense bridled. "Nonsense. Just because she's tall and dark, instead of small and fair like you. Why, Licia's as pretty in her own way as Dezzie. And I'm glad Ravenworth is smart enough to see it."

Mama hit the table with her fist in a most unladylike display of temper. The silver jumped, and so did the footmen. "Why must I be surrounded by such idiots?" she cried.

Aunt Hortense's eyes blazed. "I am not an idiot, Dorothea. Nor is your elder daughter. I think it most unkind of you to say such a thing."

Mama had the grace to look a little contrite, though not for long. "I am sorry, Hortense. But it is so maddening. I am trying to marry off Dezzie, and everyone is contriving to stop me."

"Including yourself," whispered Penelope in an undertone.

But Mama was not to be distracted. "Now, Licia, as I said, you must discourage his grace. You must—"

"No, Mama. I shall not."

"Delicia Marie Dudley!"

Dezzie got to her feet. Her knuckles whitened as she gripped the back of her chair for support. "Mama, please, listen. I do not *want* to marry the duke. I would not marry him if—if I should have to remain unwed forever."

"Nonsense," said Mama. "You shall do as I say."

Dezzie's lower lip trembled, but she went bravely on. "No, Mama, I shall not. I love Lockwood. He is the only man I shall ever marry."

Mama leapt to her feet, pushing back her chair with such force that a footman had to rush forward to catch it. "Ingrates!" Mama screamed. "Ungrateful ingrates!" And off she stormed, almost bowling over the footman as she went.

Penelope smothered a laugh in her napkin. "Sorry, Cousin. It's just . . . sometimes your mama . . ."

"I know." Licia managed a smile. Mama's tantrums could be amusing to onlookers. And she had long known that Mama thought Dezzie beautiful and herself plain. But she had never heard it said aloud before.

She turned to her aunt. "Thank you for defending me."

Aunt Hortense smiled warmly. "Your mama has no call to treat you so unfairly. And I meant what I said to her. In your own way you're every bit as pretty as Dezzie. It's easy to see why Ravenworth is taken with you. But, my dear . . ." Aunt Hortense hesitated. "He has prided himself so long on staying free. Are you sure he means to play this out to the end?"

Licia swallowed a sigh. "As sure as I can be."

Aunt Hortense seemed satisfied with that, and she finished her tea and went off, leaving the young women alone.

"Do you really love the duke?" Dezzie asked the minute her aunt was gone.

Penelope cast a glance at the footmen. "Let's take a turn in the garden."

"Do you really love the duke?" Dezzie repeated the instant they were outside.

"Of course not," replied Licia. "You know it is all part of the arrangement. So that you can wed Lockwood. Then Ravenworth and I . . ." The words did not want to come. She could hardly bear to think of that time. Why must Dezzie talk about it?

But Dezzie went rambling on, stopping here and there to examine a flower. "It's so kind of you to do this for me. And you do it so well. You look very in love. And the duke . . . he is excellent in the part. No doubt he has loved many ladies and so has had much practice."

Licia had just begun to feel the pain of this possibility when Penelope said, "No, he has not loved many ladies. Come now, stop badgering your sister."

Dezzie straightened from smelling a rose. "Oh, dear. Was I doing that? I'm sorry, Licia."

And Licia knew she was. Dezzie was flighty, but she was never deliberately unkind. "I know, dear. Run along now. I shall be fine."

When they were alone, Penelope said, "You may be able to fool the others. But not me. You do love Ravenworth."

Licia, looking out over the flowers, said dully, "Of course I don't. It's all part of—"

"Licia!" Penelope grabbed her by the shoulders and looked her directly in the eye. "I know you love him."

"No. I . . ." Suddenly Licia could keep the secret no longer. "Please, don't let him know." She wiped at her eyes. "He has done so much for us. And I . . . I should be embarrassed if he found out. Please, Penelope."

"Of course I'll keep your secret, my dear." Penelope sighed. "As you are keeping mine. But, Cousin—"

"I know! I know he doesn't believe in the institution of marriage. And he certainly doesn't love me. That hurts. But I can't end the arrangement now. At least Dezzie should have the man she loves."

By that afternoon a relative calm had settled upon the household. Aunt Hortense seemed bemused, and occasionally she gave Licia a sidelong glance or a reassuring smile. Mama, whose moods of ire seldom lasted long, once more took up her nearly unrecognizable needlepoint. And the young women sat, occupying themselves with aimless chatter.

Dezzie's eyes went so often toward the street that finally Aunt Hortense remarked on it. "Dezzie, you seem uncommonly eager for visitors."

Dezzie smiled. "I spoke to the duke about vouchers to Almack's. I was hoping he'd bring them today."

Mama nodded happily. "I'm sure if he said he would, he will. When you are duchess . . ."

Licia's heart sank. All the to-do that morning might as well have never happened. Mama was still making the same ridiculous plans.

Dezzie opened her mouth to say something, but Licia warned her off with a glance. It did not seem proper to teach her sister how to circumvent their parent, but if she was going to marry Lockwood, Dezzie would have to learn. She would have to learn to do what must be done and then let Mama's wrathful words flow past without regarding them. If she just . . .

"Listen!" Dezzie sprang to her feet. "I hear a carriage."

She ran to the window and peeked between the curtains. "It's him. It's the duke!"

Seeing Dezzie's expression turn to disappointment, Licia realized her sister had hoped to see Lockwood. But evidently Ravenworth had come alone. She tried to prepare herself to greet him calmly. But her heart was pounding so that she feared even Mama could hear it across the room.

Dezzie waited for no conventional greeting. Definitely Mama's daughter, she pounced on Ravenworth the moment he entered. "Did you get them? When are we going?"

The duke sent Licia an amused smile. "Get what, Miss Desiree?"

"Oh, you know. The vouchers for Almack's. I do so want to go."

"Why, Miss Desiree, it was only last night that you mentioned them."

"Yes, yes, but you are a duke. You can do anything."

"I am not so sure of that," he said with a sidelong glance at the other two. "But I've no doubt I can procure vouchers for Almack's."

"Oh, you are the dearest man!" And Dezzie so far forgot decorum as to throw herself into his arms. For the barest moment he appeared startled. Then he put her gently from him. "Your thanks are accepted, Miss Desiree. But I do not have the vouchers yet."

Aunt Hortense smiled. "Dezzie, do sit down and stop acting such a green girl. The duke will think you've lost your senses."

"Yes, Aunt." Dezzie sank into a chair, favoring the duke with a welcoming smile.

"Well," said Penelope. "I suppose we shall have to suffer also."

"Of course." Ravenworth crossed the room to take a chair by Licia. "I shall certainly get vouchers for you all." He gave Penelope a searching look. "So, Pen, have your calls dropped off because of last week's fiasco, that wager with Lockwood?"

"Au contraire," Penelope replied. "We have callers every day. The Duchess of Oldenburgh has been here several times. Everywhere we go, people have been delighted to receive us. Your escapade was a mere bagatelle. All the talk now is about the Russians."

Mama looked up. "Oh, yes, the dear duchess . . . she said the other night that she's going to bring her brother to call."

Aunt Hortense frowned. "I should not count on that, Dorothea. The Czar of Russia cannot be calling on—"

Mama moved fretfully. "His sister said they would come. And I believe her. She was telling me about this marvelous new dance. They call it the waltz."

"Dorothea!" Aunt Hortense raised an expressive eyebrow. "People of breeding do not indulge in that vulgar dance."

"I'm sure I don't know why," Mama insisted. "The duchess said it's wonderful fun. You go whirling around the floor at great speed. And the men hold on to the women by the waist."

"My gracious!" said Aunt Hortense. "They will never dance that at Almack's. It sounds almost . . ."

"Indecent?" suggested Ravenworth with a wink that only Licia could see.

"Yes," agreed Aunt Hortense, giving him a reluctant smile. "Indecent. And you needn't be so gleeful about it, you naughty boy. I'm sure the patronesses will never allow it."

Mama pursed her lips. "Then they will be behaving very rudely. The duchess said the waltz is the czar's most favorite dance."

Aunt Hortense shook her head. "I cannot think Lady Jersey will permit it. They are very strict about such things."

"So they are," agreed the duke. "And that reminds me . . ." He turned an eye on Dezzie, now apparently sunk in dreams of the coming event. "Miss Desiree?"

Dezzie sat up straighter. "Yes, Your Grace?"

"I must have your solemn promise that you will not dance more than twice with any man."

"Yes, Your Grace."

"And you will remember?"

"Oh, yes, Your Grace."

"Good." He returned his attention to Licia. "And now that that is settled, may I ask how you are this afternoon?"

She discovered within herself a terrible longing to tell him everything she was thinking and feeling. Instead she said, "I am well."

He frowned. "I find you're looking rather pale. Come, let us take a turn in the courtyard. With your permission, Lady Chester."

Aunt Hortense actually looked pleased. "Of course, my boy. Run along."

"Dezzie," said Mama, "don't be getting too much sun."

Dezzie got to her feet. "Yes, Mama."

At a look from Ravenworth, Penelope rose to follow. "I shall go too."

In the courtyard Penelope took Dezzie off to admire the blossoms, leaving Licia and Ravenworth alone. "Come sit on this bench." He fussed over her until she was seated, then settled beside her. "Now," he said, "you are looking pale. Has something happened to upset you?"

"No. I . . . this morning Mama tried again to . . . she just does not listen! And it is so exasperating." She sighed. "To have to do everything by deception when one is really a straightforward person. I . . . I was forced to tell her outright that . . ." She raised her eyes. She felt compelled to look into his face. "That . . . I have formed an attachment for you."

Something happened in his eyes, something she did not understand. They grew even blacker, and quite unfathomable.

"And how did she respond to this information?" he asked finally, his tone noncommittal.

"She said . . ." Now she felt the pain of Mama's words. "She said you could not possibly have any feeling for me. Because"—she hated hearing the break in her voice—"because I am not beautiful like Dezzie."

His handsome features grew grim. "That woman has so little sense. I should like to—" He recollected himself. "You must not let such observations wound you, my dear. You are, in truth, a most attractive woman."

Her laughter was so harsh that across the garden the others turned and looked at them. "Of course," she cried. "That is why the suitors have all flocked 'round my door."

"Sarcasm does not become you," he said, his voice tender. "Besides, you cannot expect anyone to compete with *me*." His disarming grin took the edge off her bleak spirits. "Your mama was right in one thing. I *am* a good catch. Ask anyone in London. They will tell you that."

She managed a smile. "I'm sure they will. And they will also laugh and shake their heads over me when Dezzie is safely wed and our arrangement is over."

He took her hand in his. "That needn't be true. After all, I am a gentleman. *You* may be the one to turn *me* off. Be assured I shall act properly wounded. That will give the dragons something to wag their tongues at. But that will not be for some time yet. We do not seem to be making much progress with your mama."

"We are making *none*," she said. "And I don't believe we ever shall."

"Come, come." He drew her arm through his. "I thought you were more light-spirited than this. Let us not succumb to a fit of the dismals. Napoleon is safely stowed away on Elba. The sun is warm, the breeze invigorating. Let us enjoy the beauty of the day."

And Licia, remembering her resolve to savor every precious moment with him, matched her smile to his and sauntered by his side through the sweet-smelling flowers to where the others waited.

10

The intervening days passed in a whirlwind of activity, and the next Wednesday night found them fighting the crush at Almack's. Licia was still battling an uncharacteristic sadness. Normally she was a bright-spirited person, even though she had so often to deal with Mama in various difficult moods.

But now, wearing a new gown only because Aunt Hortense had insisted that if Dezzie had one, she must, too, Licia felt sadly dispirited. Hanging on the duke's every word was not that difficult for her. But every second in his company she was reminded of the illusionary character of their courtship. And to be the recipient of his present favors only made the future loss of them more painful. But she had determined to do her best for Dezzie.

And besides, she hadn't the courage to end their arrangement before the necessary time. So she stood by his side with a smile as false as the paste diamonds some impecunious ladies were reputed to wear, nodding and chatting, while Mama kept giving her dark looks and pushing Dezzie toward the duke.

Finally, to Licia's great relief, the Duchess of Oldenburgh and Czar Alexander arrived. Mama left off pushing Dezzie, and scurried away to meet the emperor.

Dezzie came over to her sister. "Isn't the czar a marvelous-looking man? So straight and tall. Now that's how a ruler ought to look. You can tell *he* doesn't wear stays." She shot Ravenworth a speaking glance but he remained silent. "Look at that bright green uniform, so military, with the gold epaulets and all."

Ravenworth squeezed Licia's hand. "Why, Miss Desiree. To hear you run on so, one would think you were developing a *tendre* for the emperor."

Dezzie grinned at the man she had once feared. "You won't catch me like that, Your Grace. My heart belongs to Lockwood. And you know it."

Ravenworth smiled. "He's a lucky pup. Why, if it weren't for Licia here, I might . . ."

Dezzie's eyes widened, and for a moment she looked almost frightened. Then she laughed. "Oh, Your Grace. You caught me that time. I admit it. You shouldn't be bamming a poor girl like me. It isn't fair." Impulsively she touched his arm. "I do thank you for the vouchers. And for all you're doing to help us."

"No thanks are necessary," his grace replied. "I am quite enjoying myself." He smiled. "And so shall you, I believe. Look who has just arrived."

Dezzie hurried off to greet her Lockwood, the handsome czar forgotten.

"So," said Ravenworth. "What do you think of our famous visitor?"

Licia shrugged. She would far rather think of Ravenworth. But she could hardly tell him that, so she answered his question. "He has quite a military bearing. But his expression seems a little distant. Perhaps I am prejudiced. I do not care much for his sister, the duchess."

"Why do you suppose that is?"

She hesitated, but it was so good to be able to talk to him, be understood. "Well, for one thing she asks such personal questions. And for another, she is always quizzing Mama about that awful bed."

He was beginning to frown and she hastened to add in a

106

soothing tone, "No matter. I am used to Mama telling the story. Only usually people don't ask her to repeat it."

"That does indicate poor breeding," he agreed. He turned. "Listen, the musicians are starting to play. Shall we dance?"

The quadrille was enjoyable, and no one seemed to pay them any mind. "Good," said the duke as he looked about. "Pen was right. The Russians are the center of attention. Our escapade is old news already."

Licia smiled. "Thank goodness for that. Now if only Mama does not do some terribly embarrassing thing."

Ravenworth frowned again. "You are always worrying, my dear. One would think you the mama and her the child. You should live your life and leave your mama to her own devices."

She stared at him. "Are you suggesting"—it was hard to get the words out—"that I marry?"

He nodded. "That seems to be the only way to get free of her. I take it your papa did not leave you with anything of your own."

"Not a penny." She sighed. Should she tell him? But it would make no difference, anyway. He was not interested in marrying anyone. "He did not leave me even a dowry." She sighed. "He was such a vigorous man. And still quite young. He did not expect—"

"Quite so," said Ravenworth comfortingly. "I understand. But your mama could have provided for you. Surely she has set up a dowry for Dezzie."

"Yes, but by that time . . ." She found she was dreadfully tired of defending Mama. "Let us talk of something else," she said with another false smile.

Others came to request a dance with her. It seemed that, though it had not convinced Mama, their plan had convinced others. Many men wanted to partner the woman who had taken Ravenworth by storm. They eyed her curiously and some even asked rather penetrating questions, which, with a lifetime of dealing with Mama behind her, she was able to evade.

And every time she was returned to the sidelines Ravenworth was there waiting for her. "Why do you not dance with someone else?" she asked him finally.

Taking her hand, he gazed soulfully into her eyes. "I am so smitten by you, my dearest love, that dancing with another is meaningless."

It was almost like she was divided into two people. One of them laughed aloud at his exaggerated looks and tone. But the other was silently weeping because his words of love were uttered only in jest.

"There," he said, patting her hand. "That is somewhat better. Now give me a real smile. Why, the way you've been mooning about people will think you're unhappy with me."

If he knew what she was feeling . . . "Never, Your Grace. I—" His expression changed, grew so concerned that she asked, "What is it? What's wrong?"

He frowned. "It appears that your mama has made herself a conquest. The emperor is leading her out to the dance floor."

Licia turned to stare. "Oh, dear. Now I suppose the entire royal family will have heard the details of the celebrated bed."

Ravenworth touched her arm. "Shall I . . . but wait. By Jove, that's a waltz they're starting up. And in Almack's yet." He took her hand. "Look, there goes the Countess Lieven. Is she going to stop them? No, she's telling them to go on."

He smiled down at Licia. "It seems your Aunt Hortense was wrong. The waltz has come to Almack's. And with a vengeance."

Licia could hardly believe it. But there went Mama, whirling 'round the floor and smiling up at the Czar of Russia like the greenest girl. Trust Mama to do just as she pleased.

But the dancing did look like fun. And after the first moment of raised eyebrows and shocked whispers, other men were leading their partners onto the floor.

Ravenworth was smiling. "Come," he said. "Let us join the rest of them."

"Oh! I—" The thought of being in his arms was at once terrifying and thrilling. "Your Grace, I do not know how to waltz."

He shot his cuffs. "A minor point. It's a simple dance. I shall count it out for you. One, two, three—one, two, three. You just lean back against my hand and give yourself into my guidance."

The touch of his hand on her waist was unnerving, but soon the exhilarating rhythm of the music invaded her body. Leaning into his hand, she forgot everything but the elation of the dance. She whirled and swirled in his arms, wishing only that the dance would go on forever.

It did not, of course. All too soon they were back on the sidelines. "There, that was not so bad." He gazed at her admiringly. "That put some color in your cheeks."

She raised a hand to her heated face. "It is a most invigorating dance, Your Grace. No wonder it is well liked. But do you think it quite proper?"

He shrugged and raised an eyebrow. "I'm afraid that propriety's neither here nor there. From the look of things, the waltz has arrived. I doubt even the patronesses can stop it now."

She turned to gaze out into the throng. "I wonder if Mama—"

And there before her stood the Emperor of Russia. "Your

mother is the charming woman," he said with only the hint of an accent. "She sends me to teach you the waltz."

Ravenworth frowned. "Miss Dudley has already waltzed. With me."

The czar's smile was as cold as the Russian steppes. "Very good. Then I only need teach the finer points." And he extended his hand.

Licia hesitated. Obviously this was something Mama had arranged to get her away from the duke. Then she would send Dezzie over to enchant him. But Ravenworth looked so angry that for a moment, it almost seemed as if his wrath were real. Then she recollected herself. It was all part of the arrangement. He was pretending jealousy to advance their cause.

She did not wish to dance with anyone but Ravenworth. But to refuse the czar . . . She dropped a pat on the duke's arm and smiled brightly. "Don't be such a grouch, my dear. It isn't every day a girl can waltz with an emperor."

Surprise flickered in Ravenworth's eyes, and then he smiled, though rather grimly. "I suppose not. But I would rather it were with me."

He was certainly playing the jealous suitor to the hilt. She'd best do her part too. "La, dear," she said in that falsely bright tone so many ladies affected. "You know we've already danced twice. We don't want people to talk about us, now do we?"

His expression grew even fiercer but he said, "Of course not. That would never do."

The emperor was an excellent dancer, perhaps even a shade better than Ravenworth, but then he had had more practice.

"Your mama has led the exciting life," the emperor observed.

"Yes." If only he would just dance. The waltz did not seem

like a dance designed for conversing.

"She tells me of a Dr. Graham."

Licia felt the blood rising to her already heated cheeks. "He is no longer with us."

"Regrettable," observed the emperor. "His celebrated bed would be a boon to certain royal houses. One's line must be preserved, you know."

"Yes, Your Highness." To think that an emperor would believe such balderdash!

His eyes grew speculative. "You belong to the fierce one from whose side I took you?"

Her heart rose up in her throat, but she managed to say, "Perhaps, Your Highness."

He smiled, a charming smile that suddenly made him more human. "You have no need for worrying. That one, he fears losing you."

She forced herself to smile. Ravenworth would have made a good actor. He had convinced the emperor, at least.

"For one in love you are too sad." Alexander frowned. "You are not sure you wish his attentions? If you wish them not, I shall turn him away. Tell him to leave you."

"Oh, no!" The prospect was so frightening that she clutched at his arm and almost missed a step.

Alexander shook his head. "Woman! I do not understand. This duke—you say you wish his attentions. He gives them. He is so jealous, he frowns like the fiercest wild boar. But still you are not happy."

She sighed. "It's a difficult story, Your Highness. My mama, she does not approve."

"How so? He has the bad reputation? No funds? Many mistr—"

"No," Licia hastened to interrupt. "It is only that she wishes him to marry my sister." A glimmer of hope had begun to shine in her mind. If the czar talked to Mama . . .

"He will never wed that little one." He smiled at her look of surprise. "Oh, yes, your mama acquainted us. The little one has lost her heart to some youth who looks ill."

Licia chuckled. Talking to the emperor was raising her spirits. "He's not really ill," she explained. "It is just the fashion to look pale since Byron wrote *Childe Harold*."

"Strange people, the English." Alexander smiled again. "The fierce one, he has made the right choice. You are the better for a wife. You have the wit as well as the beauty."

She felt the blood rushing to her cheeks again. If only Ravenworth thought that. "Your Highness is very kind."

"No, not kind. Truthful. You are beautiful woman, so beautiful that if you did not love him, I would ask . . . But you do, so I say no more on this subject. Tell me, what do the English say about land reform? It is a subject I am fond of discussing. And your mama tells me you know much about it."

When they finished the dance, he returned her to Ravenworth, bowing and kissing her hand. "Most enjoyable, thank you. I shall speak to your mama."

Ravenworth's frown grew fiercer. "Speak to your mama? About what?"

She found it hard to look into his eyes. What if her own gave away her secret? But then she remembered that he would think it only acting. "Please, Your Grace, there is no need to glare so. He . . . he simply observed that you seemed jealous. And he offered to persuade you from your attentions to me. But I said no, that I welcomed them."

His frown began to smooth itself out. "And your mama?"

"I . . . I told him she stood in our way. And he offered to speak to her."

The duke's frown was coming back, and she hastened on. "It might help. You know how Mama is about nobility."

"You didn't tell him it was all a ruse?"

"Of course not. He might tell Mama."

"Very well." He smiled ruefully. "But I find I don't like the man, though I'm not sure why."

To her surprise she found herself saying, "I found him rather charming. But perhaps that was because he told me that I am beautiful."

For a moment she thought his frown would return in full force. But then he composed his features and asked, "Why do you believe him and not me?" He offered her his arm. "No matter. My throat is abominably dry. Shall we have some warm lemonade?"

The dancing was almost at an end when Alexander presented himself again. "With your permission . . ." he said to Ravenworth.

The duke glowered but he nodded, and Licia followed the emperor to the floor.

"He is bad in love," observed Alexander. "He looks to skewer me with the sword."

She managed a chuckle. "He has been long on the town, Your Highness. And I am the first . . ." She flushed at the lie she wished with her whole heart were true.

Alexander nodded. "Ah, yes, the first to capture his heart. Well, I soon return you to him. But first I tell you. I speak to your mama." He shook his head. "She is strange woman. She tell me the duke marries your sister. I tell her is not true. I know is not true. She does not hear me. She tells me about wedding day."

He frowned. "I think when time comes, you just go to him. You have no papa, no brothers. There would be no duel. You marry him and be happy."

If only she could. Her eyes filled with tears, and the lump

in her throat made speech difficult. Still, she had to try. "Thank you, Your Highness. I appreciate your efforts with Mama."

"That is all right. I am sorry I do not succeed." He returned her to Ravenworth and had hardly left them before the duke demanded, "Well?"

She shook her head. "Mama did not listen. She is planning your wedding day. Yours and Dezzie's."

His eyebrows met in a fierce, dark line. "That woman! How did you ever manage—" He struggled to control himself. "I'm sorry, my dear. You've enough trouble with that mama of yours. You don't need to listen to my diatribes."

She gave him a soothing smile. "It's all right, Your Grace. I know Mama is very trying on the nerves."

"Did he said anything else?"

She hesitated. "He . . . he suggested that the best way to convince her would be for us . . . to marry. But that is out of the question, of course."

His eyes grew darker. "Of course."

For a long moment he stared at her, then he shook himself as though shaking off some unpleasant thought. "Come, let us see if we can find Pen."

11

It was several days later that Penelope asked, "Licia, will you help me?"

They were alone in the room but Licia hesitated. She did not wish to carry any more messages to Harry Bates. She found that more and more she could understand Penelope's feelings, but this clandestine message carrying made her frightfully nervous. "What is it you wish me to do?"

Penelope sighed. "I want to get Mama to the gallery. I want her to make Harry's acquaintance."

"Penelope! You're not—"

Penelope smiled sadly. "Of course I'm not going to tell her what he means to me. I just want them to meet each other."

"Isn't that . . . rather dangerous?"

Penelope shrugged. "Perhaps, but if Mama disowns me, Harry will be *forced* to marry me. At any rate, I must do something. I cannot wait forever."

Licia nodded. "Yes, well. Tell me what you want me to do."

So it was that afternoon found them at Turner's Gallery. Aunt Hortense frowned as she stepped down from the carriage. "I truly do not see what is so difficult about choosing a painting for me," she said to Penelope. "You have never been one to shillyshally about such things. You had no such trouble when you purchased the Constable."

"I know, Mama," Penelope said soothingly. "But then I knew exactly which one you should prefer. This is quite a different case."

Licia swallowed a sigh. Penelope was treading on very dangerous ground. And to what purpose? Even if Aunt Hortense liked Harry, it would not be in the role of son-in-law. She could not imagine Aunt Hortense allowing her daughter to marry an artist of any kind.

Penelope escorted her mama inside, and the others followed.

"So many pictures," Mama said plaintively, "but they are all of the country. Doesn't the man like the city?"

"I don't know, Mama." Dezzie led her off, peering into every dark corner, as though she expected to conjure up Lockwood.

And Penelope was growing paler every second. It seemed strange that her mama did not notice it. Harry Bates came down the room to greet them, and Licia felt herself grow weak. If she felt so, how much more Penelope must feel the tension of this moment. Was her cousin going to get through this meeting without giving away her secret?

"Mama," Penelope said, "this is Mr. Bates, Mr. Turner's assistant. He has kindly been helping me with the paintings. Mr. Bates, this is my mother, Lady Chester."

Harry looked nervous too. His face was pale and his lower lip had a tendency to tremble. But the feelings of inferiors were beneath the notice of a lady. Aunt Hortense merely nodded. "Show me the paintings," she said crisply. "I'll soon have the matter settled."

When she surveyed *Hannibal Crossing the Alps*, she chuckled. "Eglantine's boy is right. Hannibal's hardly visible. But that is quite a magnificent storm. Look at how the clouds are roiling about. Where's the other?"

"Here, Mama," Penelope said. Licia detected the tremor in her cousin's voice, but her aunt seemed oblivious to it.

While Penelope's mama was occupied with studying the

sunlight breaking through the clouds onto Calais Pier, Licia watched her cousin smile tenderly at Harry Bates and receive a smile in return. Why must it be so difficult for them? They were not asking for such a horrible thing—just the chance to be together.

"Well," said Aunt Hortense, turning to Harry. "Which painting do you think the better?"

Harry smiled tentatively. "I believe I prefer the *Hannibal*, milady. See how Turner has used the circular swirl of the storm rather than the verticals and horizontals we artists traditionally employ. He shows the majesty of nature reducing men to utter insignificance."

Aunt Hortense frowned. "I am not sure I care to be considered insignificant."

Penelope blanched, and Harry straightened as though to defend his statements. But Aunt Hortense went on. "Tell me about the other. What is unusual about it?"

Harry swallowed. Obviously he was feeling the strain. "*Calais Pier*," he said, "is different because instead of showing the waves as dark blue or green, the master makes them peak and swell, raging in a white froth."

He pointed with his forefinger. "Notice how the pier tapers sharply, leading the eye to the horizon and from there up to the clouds where the sun is breaking through."

Aunt Hortense nodded thoughtfully. "Yes, I see. And what do you feel is the meaning of this one?"

Harry shifted from one foot to the other. "Meaning, milady?"

Aunt Hortense eyed him shrewdly. "Yes, meaning. If the *Hannibal* shows nature reducing men to insignificance, what does this one show?"

Harry's response was immediate. "Man's bravery, milady. Bravery in adversity. These fishermen are setting out in the face of the storm with great determination because it is what they must do."

His glance slid over Penelope, and she nodded emphatically, but Aunt Hortense was too deep in thought to notice.

"Yes," she said finally. "I can see that in this painting. Thank you, Mr. Yates."

"Bates, Mama," Penelope said, hastening to correct her.

Aunt Hortense shrugged. "Yates, Bates. No matter."

"But his name—"

Aunt Hortense stared at her daughter. "How many times must I tell you? The man is a tradesman. It matters little to him what we call him, as long as we buy."

Harry Bates reddened but remained silent.

Penelope did not. "But—"

Licia laid a restraining hand on her cousin's arm. "So, Aunt, which painting is to be your choice?"

Thus distracted, Aunt Hortense forgot the subject of names. "I'm going to purchase *Calais Pier*." She nodded to Harry. "Wrap it up and send it along."

"Very well, milady."

Licia could feel Penelope trembling. She smiled at her sympathetically and willed her to remain silent.

"Come along now, Dorothea, Dezzie," Aunt Hortense called. "If I'm not mistaken, the Duchess of Oldenburgh means to call today. You know you'll be up in the boughs if we are not home to receive her."

They had just gotten in the front door and removed their bonnets when the sound of a carriage sent Dezzie rushing to look. "It's the duke!" she cried. "And he's brought his mama. And the Duchess of Oldenburgh."

"Well, let us go into the drawing room," said Aunt Hortense. "I'll ring for some refreshments."

Licia followed, her knees trembling. She had not seen Ravenworth since their visit to Almack's. But she thought of him constantly—of his kindness, of his attentions to her.

She wanted Dezzie to wed her Lockwood. But when that happened, when Mama was finally convinced, then Mama and she would return to the country. She would not see much of Ravenworth. Oh, perhaps he would still be her friend, as he was Penelope's friend. But there was no denying it. She did not want Ravenworth as a friend. What she had said to Mama was the truth. She wanted Ravenworth as a husband.

She settled into a damask-covered chair and took her needlepoint from its basket. But immediately she put it down again. The way she was feeling, her stitching would be as unrecognizable as Mama's. And the house in York was already overflowing with that sort.

"Come in, come in," said Aunt Hortense as the visitors appeared in the doorway.

The dowager duchess paused. "This is not a social call. We have come on important business."

Licia's breath stopped in her throat and her hands gripped the hard wooden arms of the chair. Ravenworth had not mentioned such a visit. He couldn't have come to . . . no, it must be something else.

Aunt Hortense looked a little surprised. "Well, then, suppose you tell us with whom you have this business."

The duchess chuckled and smiled at her friend. "It is difficult to say exactly. You see, the business is David's. And it is with Mrs. Dudley." She sent Licia a comforting, warm smile as she crossed the room and took a seat. "The duchess and I have come along, to play the advocate should he need us."

Licia's heart began to thud madly. He did mean to . . .

Aunt Hortense looked to the duke and smiled. "Do you wish privacy, Your Grace?"

Crossing to the fireplace, he leaned against the mantelpiece. He raised a dark eyebrow. "That hardly seems possible now. Everyone in London knows that I have been often seen with Miss Dudley. Miss Licia Dudley."

Mama opened her mouth, but the duke did not permit her to speak. He bowed toward her and said firmly, "I know, Madame, that this is not the way you wished it to occur. But I have formed an intense attachment for Miss Dudley. And I wish . . ."

He paused, and Licia, realizing that her knuckles had turned white, loosened her grip on the arms of the chair and carefully moved her hands to her lap. He was not going to be able to say it. The lie would stick in his throat. And no wonder—a man who could not stand the institution of marriage saying that he wished to marry.

"I wish to court your elder daughter formally," Ravenworth continued, and to her surprise the words rang out loud and clear. "And eventually I wish to make Licia my duchess."

Mama frowned. "But Your Grace, surely you can see that Dezzie would make you the better wife. She is younger and prettier."

The Duchess of Oldenburgh snorted. "Foolishness," she said, giving Mama a haughty look. "The elder daughter is the beauty. My brother, he says so. And Alexander—he knows the beautiful woman."

Ravenworth frowned. It must be irksome for him to have to do this at all. And to have to do so publicly made it even worse.

He pulled himself to his full height and turned a stern eye on Mama. "I feel constrained to tell you, Mrs. Dudley, that if you do not grant me permission to court Licia, I shall take the first opportunity to run off with her."

Aunt Hortense dropped her fan with a clatter. Penelope shot her cousin a searching look. And Mama gasped. "Your Grace, you wouldn't!"

But the duke stood firm, every inch the lord. "I would indeed. For I intend to have her, one way or another."

"My dear Dorothea," said the dowager duchess in a placating tone. "I know this is somewhat of a shock to you. But believe me, my son means what he says. I have never seen him so adamant upon any matter." She gave Mama a sweet smile. "Besides, you will still have Ravenworth in your family. And just think, a daughter of yours wed to a duke!"

"And if you play your cards right, another to a viscount," said his grace.

Mama sent him a sharp glance.

"Yes," he said. "Let me woo Licia. And let Lockwood woo Dezzie."

"Well, I never." Mama looked almost stunned. "I never would have believed it, Licia with a duke." She sent the Duchess of Oldenburgh a bewildered glance. "He said that? Alexander said Licia is a beauty?"

The duchess nodded emphatically. "He admires her greatly. She talks to him of land reform, of things to which he has given his heart."

"But he said she was a beauty?"

"This is so. And this marriage he approves of very much."

Licia found she was twisting her hands together in her lap. It was all very well to pretend like this, for Dezzie's sake. And she certainly appreciated Alexander's help. But she hadn't counted on so many people getting involved. When the day of reckoning came, when she had to announce that she was not becoming a duchess, Mama would be properly incensed. And it would be Licia who remained to listen to the complaints— for many, many days. Still, if it would ensure Dezzie's happiness, she would be glad to do it.

"So," his grace was saying, "you will give Lockwood permission to call on Dezzie?"

"Yes, yes. He is your nephew, after all." Mama smiled. "And when shall you wed Licia, Your Grace? Oh, I can hardly wait to start planning it. Imagine, a great wedding for Licia."

Licia saw the shadow that crossed his face. Even the pretense of a wedding was painful to him.

"We have not gotten that far, Madame. I wished your consent before I spoke to Licia."

"Well, well, you have it." Mama smiled happily and turned to the others. "I always knew my Licia would do well in life. After all, Dr. Graham promised . . ."

The duke took a step toward her. His eyebrows met in the center of his forehead and his frown was ferocious to behold. Never had Licia seen him look so forbidding. "Mrs. Dudley—" he began.

"You must call me Mama now." Evidently Mama saw nothing amiss.

"I believe I shall reserve that privilege until after our nuptials."

"Well, if you must, but—"

"Mrs. Dudley, please. You must listen to me."

Mama stopped and Ravenworth pulled in a deep breath. "I must beg that you desist from speaking of that infamous bed," he said. "Ever again."

Mama frowned. "Why, Dr. Graham's bed was perfectly proper. I was there with Mr. Dudley, wasn't I? I'm sure—"

"He is right," pronounced the Duchess of Oldenburgh solemnly. "Such talk is not good. People laugh." She sent Ravenworth a sympathetic glance. "His grace does not wish people should laugh at his duchess."

Mama considered this in puzzlement but finally she

nodded. "Very well. I shall mention it no more. But I think you're all quite ridiculous." She turned to her sister. "Now, Hortense, who is the best modiste in London? We must think about . . ."

Ravenworth crossed the room to Licia. "Perhaps you'll walk with me in the courtyard," he said, his smile warm and inviting.

"Of course." She wanted nothing more than to get away from Mama's empty babbling. A wedding gown that would never be worn and probably the most grandiose feast the city had ever seen but which, of course, would never be served.

The door had barely closed behind them when Ravenworth grabbed her 'round the waist and whirled her in a great, exuberant circle. "We have done it!" he cried. "We have actually changed your mama's mind!"

"Your Grace, please! You are making me quite dizzy."

He looked instantly contrite and set her carefully on her feet. "My dear, I am sorry. In my excitement I was carried away. But do you think it went well?"

"Yes." Still dizzy, she clung to him, her head against his shoulder. She even laughed a little. "Very well. And now you have Mama in your pocket. You will soon find that she meant you for me from the beginning."

His eyebrows rose. "I shall find what?"

She nodded. "Oh, yes. Mama will insist it was all her idea."

He smiled and shrugged. "Then we shall take care not to disabuse her of the notion."

He offered her his arm and she leaned on it gratefully as they strolled on among the blossoms. "But," she continued, trying to keep talking, trying not to remember his arms around her, "you did surprise me with that talk of running off. Why, what should you have done if Mama still did not consent? We could not possibly have run off."

He frowned and his eyes darkened. "No, I suppose not. But I thought perhaps mention of it would touch her heart. Because of your father."

"Perhaps it did. With Mama it is very hard to say."

He smiled. "I apologize for making the thing into a raree-show, bringing along my own performing troupe like that. But when I told Mama what I planned, she said . . ."

A thought occurred to her. "Did you tell your mama of the ruse?"

"I—I told her the truth."

She had always liked his mother. "She is a very kind lady. To go to so much trouble for Dezzie."

"Yes." He looked slightly troubled.

"What is it? Did she disapprove of our arrangement?"

"No."

There was still something strange about his expression. "What did she say when you told her?"

"She . . . ah . . . cautioned me not to tell anyone else."

"So the Duchess of Oldenburgh doesn't know the truth."

"Good Lord, no!"

"Good. It wouldn't be wise. If Mama should find out that we have tricked her"—she shook her head—"she would be very angry."

He smiled at her. "Do not worry. She will not discover it."

"Perhaps not. But she will discover that I am not to be a duchess. I do not look forward to that day, I can tell you."

His smile broadened. "Truly? And why not?"

She stared at him. How could he ask such a question? "Because Mama will put all the blame on me."

He picked a white rosebud and offered it to her. "You worry too much, my dear. That time is still far off."

"But it is coming." She sniffed the rose's sweet fragrance

before she forced herself to ask the question that had been clamoring in her mind. "How long do you think we should wait before . . . before . . ."

"Before you drive me from your side?" His smile took the sting from his words. "Are you that eager to be rid of my company?"

His eyes were searching her face and she felt a blush rising. "Oh, no, Your Grace. Your company is most delightful, as you well know. It is just that . . . well, in dancing attendance on me you are neglecting your other social duties. Your friends, your other female acquaintances . . ."

His expression grew sober. "I have no social duties except those I wish to have. My friends at White's are laying wagers on the date of my becoming leg-shackled. And the frail ones"—he sent her a penetrating look—"The frail ones see me no more."

"Your Grace, I did not mean—"

His gloved hand lay comfortingly upon hers. "Licia, you are not a child. You know the ways of the city. I am a man of six and thirty. I have been on the town for many years. Naturally I have had my share of ladies. But since I have been paying court to you, I have forsaken my old pursuits."

Her heart began to thud in her breast. Could he really mean what he was saying? Could it be that he really cared? But common sense would not allow her to believe such a thing. She struggled to keep her tone light. "Really, Your Grace. Did you need to go to such lengths?"

He frowned. "I am a man of honor. I would not wish to do anything that might reflect on your good name."

She sighed. "That was most kind of you. But you have done so much for us. And in return we have disrupted the even tenor of your life. You have undertaken a project that can only be distasteful to you."

He chuckled. "Do not make it sound like such a terrible thing. I have quite enjoyed myself. And I shall go on doing so long as our arrangement continues."

And with that she had to be content.

❋ *12* ❋

It was not until the next afternoon that Penelope brought the conversation 'round, in a circuitous fashion, to Harry Bates. They were sitting in the drawing room while Mama attempted to teach Dezzie the finer techniques of needlepoint. Given Mama's proven inadequacies in such matters Licia might have found the subject amusing. But now she was far too worried about her cousin. Since the previous day Penelope had been acting quite strangely.

Now her cousin looked up from her project and cast a worried look at her mother. "Tell me, Mama, why did you choose *Calais Pier* rather than *Hannibal* at the gallery yesterday?"

Aunt Hortense sighed. "I suppose it's because I liked the effect of the sunlight breaking through the clouds like that. It is basically a hopeful picture. And I am a hopeful person." She smiled at Licia. "Today I am particularly cheerful for Licia's sake. Imagine Ravenworth's marrying! I never thought to see the day Ravenworth would marry anyone."

"Nor I, Mama," said Penelope with an encouraging smile to her cousin. "But even David was not proof against Cupid's arrows."

Aunt Hortense chuckled. "I daresay it was the land reform that did it, with maybe a little help from Alexander."

"But Aunt—"

"Nonsense," Aunt Hortense said. "I know a jealous man when I see one. I expect he'll be clamoring for a wedding date quite soon."

Licia could only nod and remain silent. She much disliked

deceiving her aunt. Aunt Hortense was a kind person who clearly had her niece's welfare in mind. But the deception could not be avoided. There was no other way to help Dezzie.

"And what did you think of Mr. Bates?" Penelope inquired.

Taken by surprise, Licia stabbed her finger with the needle and bit her lip to keep back a cry.

"Who?" asked Aunt Hortense.

Penelope looked stricken, and Licia rushed to say, "The young man who helped you with the pictures."

Aunt Hortense shrugged. "He seemed to have a sound mind. Certainly he was good at talking about the paintings."

"I heard . . ." Penelope faltered, then, with visible effort, pulled herself together and went on. "I heard that he and a lady are considering marriage."

Aunt Hortense didn't even look up. "Impossible," she said, taking another stitch. "No lady would stoop that low."

Licia tried to signal to Penelope to stop talking, but though she saw her, her cousin ignored her efforts.

"I don't see what's so low about it," Penelope said. "He looks personable enough, and you just said he has a sound mind."

"And no doubt an empty pocket." Aunt Hortense frowned. "A woman may marry up." She looked at Licia. "But she should not marry down."

"I married down," said Mama into the silence. "And I have never regretted it."

"Of course you haven't," Aunt Hortense continued reasonably. "Still, it should not be done."

Mama shook her head. "Those rules are set down by the ton. What do such people know about love?"

Licia stared, her needlework forgotten. Imagine Mama saying something with which she could so heartily agree.

"Mama is right, Aunt Hortense. I . . . I should love Ravenworth if he had nothing at all."

"Nonsense," said Aunt Hortense. "That sort of silliness sounds good, but it is simply not true. If he were not a duke, Ravenworth would not be the same man at all."

"Perhaps you are right, Mama." Penelope seemed to have recovered her poise. "But money and title are not everything. And I firmly believe love may exist without either."

Aunt Hortense shrugged. "You are free to believe what you choose. I only say that no respectable woman would allow her daughter to marry such a man."

Penelope's face paled and her knuckles whitened as she dug her nails into her palms. Afraid of what might follow, Licia acted quickly. She crossed the room to stand before her cousin, thus effectively blocking her from Aunt Hortense's view. "Penelope, dear, I am thinking of changing my hairstyle. Could you spare a few minutes to give me your opinion?"

Tears brimmed in Penelope's eyes, but she made a brave effort and murmured, "Yes, Cousin. Of course."

Penelope managed to hold back the tears until they reached her room. Then she threw herself upon the great bed and began to sob. Licia gave the door a push and hurried to her side. "Penelope, my dear, come now. You must not take on so."

Penelope made a valiant effort. "I . . . I cannot help it. It is all so terrible. Mama does not see Harry, not as a real person. He is like a footman, existing only to serve her."

"Aunt Hortense is wrong," Licia admitted. "But it is not her fault. She was raised to believe as she does."

Penelope sniffed. "So was I."

Licia allowed herself a small smile. "That's right, you

were. And no doubt you would still be believing that very thing if you hadn't fallen in love with Harry Bates."

"Harry Bates!" From the half opened doorway came Dezzie's cry of dismay.

Licia grabbed her by the arm and pulled her inside, slamming the door. "What are you doing here?"

Dezzie frowned and rubbed her arm. "Penelope looked ill," she said plaintively. "I came to see if I could help. I went first to your room. And when you weren't there, I came here." She plopped down on the bed. "So you are in love with that nice Mr. Bates."

"Yes."

Dezzie frowned. "Oh, dear. Aunt Hortense will not like this above half. What was that she said about artists a while back? They are worse than—"

"Dezzie"—Licia grabbed her sister by the arm—"that is quite enough!"

Dezzie removed her arm and rubbed it again. "You mustn't be so rough," she exclaimed. "I like him," Dezzie continued. "He seems quite nice."

"He is." Penelope sniffled again. "He really is."

"Well, then," said Dezzie, "you must stick to your guns. Run off with him if need be."

"Dezzie!"

Dezzie turned. "Really, Licia. Ravenworth said he would do that if Mama forbade your courtship. And Lockwood and I . . . we have considered it, if all else should fail."

Licia shook her head. "You must not do such a thing!"

"Licia, calm down." Penelope sat up and managed a weak smile. "Neither of you will ever need Gretna Green. But I expect—nay, I hope—I shall see it someday. And soon."

Licia sighed. "Is there no other recourse?"

Penelope shook her head. "I'm afraid not. Mama seldom

changes her mind." She turned to Dezzie. "You must not tell a soul about this."

"Of course not. But why can't the duke fix it?"

"Dezzie! The duke does not know. This is a secret."

Dezzie looked at her sister. "You are keeping a secret like this from his grace? Oh, Licia, how can you do such a thing?"

"It is not my secret," Licia explained. "Nor is it yours. You must not tell a soul. Not even Lockwood."

"Oh, dear." Dezzie frowned. "That will be difficult. We have promised, you see, to tell each other everything."

Penelope nodded. "Yes, dear, I understand. But this will only be for a short time, until we can make our plans." She took Dezzie's hands in her own. "Will you help us?"

"Oh, yes," Dezzie cried, her face lighting up. "You know I will do anything to advance the cause of love."

And true to her word, Dezzie did. She kept quite silent on the subject of love. But she went about the house with a glimmer in her eye and smile on her face. Since Dezzie had never in her life been able to keep a secret, Licia was understandably nervous.

And when Lockwood called the next afternoon to take them driving, and Dezzie talked him into taking them to the gallery by saying, "Licia is interested in a painting," Licia feared the worst.

"Which painting is it?" Lockwood asked as the carriage moved away. "Old Turner's a rare sport. Those storms of his are so real."

Licia nodded. "Yes, but I prefer his quiet country scenes. I had thought to purchase *Frosty Morning*, but unfortunately someone was there before me."

A strange look crossed Lockwood's face.

"What is it?" Dezzie asked.

"Nothing. Nothing, my dear."

Dezzie pouted prettily. "Now, Lockwood, that isn't so. I know you. And something is amiss. I know! It's about that painting Licia wanted."

"Dezzie, do be sensible." Lockwood pulled nervously at his cravat. "No one knows who bought—"

"*You* know!"

Looking at the viscount's expression, Licia decided Dezzie was right. Lockwood looked extremely uncomfortable.

"Tell us," Dezzie begged.

"I . . . ah . . . can't."

Licia took pity on the young man. "Dezzie, you must stop badgering the poor man. If the viscount is not supposed to tell, you must not expect him to."

"But we promised not to keep secrets from each other."

The carriage pulled up outside the gallery. Lockwood hastened to help Dezzie down. As he did so Penelope sent Licia a pleading look. Licia took the cue. "Dezzie," she said, "you know that sometimes secrets are necessary."

Dezzie nodded. "Yes, I know. I shan't bother the viscount anymore."

Licia and Penelope both sighed in relief and followed Dezzie through the door that Lockwood opened.

Licia found her hands trembling. Harry Bates was coming down the room, and Penelope's look of eagerness was a dead giveaway. "Dezzie, go show the viscount the paintings you like. Down at the other end."

Fortunately Dezzie was quick to grasp the reason for this and hurried Lockwood off. And just in time. Harry Bates reached them and took Penelope's hands in his. "My dearest," he whispered.

Embarrassment washed over Licia. They were the only occupants of the place, so her cousin was in no danger of discovery. But the tender looks on their faces, their joy at seeing each other . . . it almost seemed wrong for any outsider to observe such deep emotions.

"Oh, Harry," Penelope cried. "I have missed you so. Harry, please, we must do something. I cannot bear it."

"Penelope, we have been over this so many times. I cannot afford a wife."

Penelope's voice turned bitter. "You mean, you cannot afford a wife like me."

"My dear, your mama—"

"My mama doesn't understand. Harry, you must agree to us running away. Ask Mr. Turner for some time off. We'll go to Gretna Green. And come back married."

Harry Bates paled. "But, Penelope, your good name, your family . . ."

Penelope laughed so harshly that Licia, afraid they had heard, glanced toward Dezzie. But the young people were engrossed with each other.

"My good name means nothing to me without you." Penelope's eyes grew wild and her voice began to tremble. "You are my family. If you will not marry me, I'll end all this misery. The bridge should—"

"Penelope!"

"Licia, I cannot help it. I have waited all my life to love a man. And now, am I to lose him because he paints pictures while members of the ton run around like naughty boys tipping over the poor Charlies in their boxes or gaming away all their substance? That's not fair."

Licia turned to Harry. "Really, Mr. Bates. Penelope has a point. Perhaps, if the marriage were accomplished, Aunt Hortense would come 'round." She was not at all certain of this, but given Penelope's distraught looks, it seemed the best thing to say.

Harry shook his head. "Lady Chester is a proud woman. She will never welcome a painter into her family."

Licia was constrained to agree with him, but she did so only to herself. Penelope deserved a chance at happiness. "We cannot know that for certain," Licia continued. "Gretna Green seems your only choice."

Harry frowned. "It is so underhanded. Why can't I just march up and proclaim my love?"

Penelope shook her head. "Because Mama would take steps. No. We cannot tell her till the deed is done."

And then, thought Licia, the fur would fly. But still, she considered an elopement their best hope, if they could get away without being stopped.

"Oh, no!" Licia clapped a hand over her mouth.

"What is it?" Penelope asked.

"When Aunt Hortense finds out, she will send someone after you. She will send Ravenworth!"

Penelope nodded. "I have thought of that. You must delay him."

"I?" Her heart went cold with fear. He could not approve of this. "How?"

"We will figure something out." Penelope turned to Harry. "Let's plan for early next week."

Harry looked unhappy but he nodded. Like her, he was probably worried about Penelope's state of mind.

The drive home was enlivened by Dezzie's chatter, but when the viscount left them at the house on Grosvenor Square, the three young women climbed the stairs in silence.

Dezzie followed the others into Penelope's room. "Is it settled, then? Have you set the date?"

Penelope sighed. "Next week. I don't know which day."

Dezzie smiled. "It is all so exciting. And guess what?"

"What?" asked Licia, more from habit than from interest.

"I know who bought *Frosty Morning*."

Licia whirled. "Dezzie, you didn't tell—"

"Of course not. Besides, the viscount doesn't know that *I* have a secret."

"And he had better not learn," Licia said sternly.

"Oh, I shan't tell. But don't you want to know?"

"Know what?"

Dezzie stamped her foot impatiently. "Who bought the painting, of course."

"Mr. Bates said the buyer didn't wish to be known."

"Well, Lockwood knows him. And so do we."

Penelope raised an eyebrow. "We do?"

"Yes." Dezzie's smile was triumphant. "The painting was purchased by Ravenworth."

Licia's breath left her body. "Whatever for?"

"Lockwood says he bought it for a woman."

Blindly Licia groped for a chair and sank into it.

"He couldn't," Penelope said firmly. "It would ruin our arrangement."

Dezzie shook her head. "Oh, no. The gallery is keeping it for him. He's not going to give it to her until he's free." Dezzie gave a little skip. "Well, I guess I'll go talk to Mama about my wedding gown. I want it to be just right." And out she went, entirely oblivious to what she had done.

Licia, staring into space, wished only for a hole to hide in.

"That Dezzie," Penelope said. "Sometimes I could choke her."

"She means no harm," Licia said dully. "She thinks it's all a farce. As it really is."

Penelope glowered. "I should like to choke David, too. Can't the man see what he's doing to you?"

Licia turned tearful eyes to her cousin. "Do not blame

him, Penelope. It is all my fault. I knew when we asked him that—that I had a *tendre* for him. He is not to blame that my attachment grew. He meant only to help us."

"Perhaps." Penelope looked thoughtful. "I wonder who this woman is."

"Please, Penelope," Licia begged. "Do not embarrass me further by trying to find out. Ravenworth has done a great deal for us. He is entitled to his privacy."

The more Licia thought about the coming elopement, the more it preyed upon her mind. It simply was not right for Penelope to have to run off like that. If only there were something she could do about it.

Ravenworth would know what to do. She could not divulge Penelope's secret to him. But maybe she could make it a hypothetical case. They had had many hypothetical discussions about land reform and other matters. But first she had to have a chance. She had to delay the elopement.

So at bedtime that night she went to Penelope's room.

Penelope looked almost as pale as her nightdress. "Come in," she said. "And close the door. I am trying to decide what to take with me."

"Oh, please, don't do it."

Penelope shook her head. "I must."

The tears came, and Licia did not try to stop them. "I—just—cannot—do this alone," she said, sobbing. "If you run off, your mama will be a veritable dragon. Ravenworth will fly up in the boughs. Mama will go wild if he leaves me now. And Dezzie and Lockwood will lose their chance. I simply cannot carry it all alone."

Penelope looked troubled. "Oh, Cousin, I am sorry. I've been so embroiled in my own problems that I have quite forgotten yours."

"Could you just wait a little while, till Dezzie's safely married? Then it won't matter if Ravenworth is upset with me."

Penelope sank down on the bed. "How long do you think it will be?"

"Perhaps August, perhaps sooner." Her heart sank at the thought of losing Ravenworth, but she forced herself to go on. "You know Harry loves you."

Penelope nodded. "Yes, and he is not at all eager to take this way out." She sighed. "Truthfully, neither am I. But I can see no other."

Licia nodded. "At least he loves you. But tell me, Penelope, will you do this for me? Will you wait?"

"Till August or Dezzie's wedding, whichever comes first," her cousin agreed. "But no longer."

"Oh, Penelope, thank you. I truly could not have managed alone."

❋ 13 ❋

The summer days passed quickly. June became July, and still Licia could think of no way to help Penelope. The city was agog with victory celebrations. After his defeat of Napoleon the great Wellington had returned to universal acclaim. And the Prince Regent, in gratitude, had made him a duke.

One Wednesday night in late July the hero appeared at Almack's. Mama was ecstatic. "Just look!" she cried, grabbing Ravenworth's arm. "There is the great man. Oh, Your Grace, do make me known to him."

Licia shuddered. "Mama, you must not ask such—"

Ravenworth shushed her. "It's all right, my dear. It's the least I can do for your mama."

His eyes twinkled, but Licia did not feel like smiling. Why did he persist in treating Mama like an ordinary person? Didn't he understand how ridiculously she could behave? How she might embarrass him? Licia was used to it, more or less. But Ravenworth was a peer.

Naturally there was a crush around the great man, but way was made for Ravenworth. Soon they were face-to-face with the hero.

"Ravenworth!" Wellington's delight showed on his face. It was a strong face, dominated by a hawkish nose and eyes that spoke of power.

"Glad to see you safely home," said Ravenworth.

"And your wound?" Wellington inquired.

"Completely healed. It's kind of you to ask. You did a tremendous job putting it over on Boney like that."

Wellington nodded. "Sometimes I wasn't at all sure we'd do it. But enough of that. Who are these lovely ladies?"

Mama tittered like a schoolgirl, and Licia flushed.

"This," said Ravenworth, drawing her forward, "is Miss Licia Dudley."

"Ah-ha!" Wellington chuckled. "At last I have seen the miracle worker. The woman who snared the unsnarable Ravenworth."

Ravenworth laughed. "You needn't find it so delightful. As I recall, you have been leg-shackled for some time."

"True, true."

"And this is Licia's mother, Mrs. Dudley."

"Enchanted," said Wellington, and gave Mama a warm smile. "Perhaps, Madame, you would care to dance with me?"

"Oh, Your Grace! Yes! I should love to. Oh, my!"

With a smile to his friend, Wellington led Mama away. "So said," Ravenworth, "we are alone at last."

"And Mama is with Wellington."

He frowned. "You worry too much."

"And if she tells him about the bed?"

To her surprise the duke merely shrugged. "He's heard far worse things than that. He'd probably enjoy it."

Licia let the subject go. If he didn't care, she would not worry about it. For days now she'd been looking for a way to ask him about Penelope's problem without him guessing it was *her* problem. Now she believed she had found a chance. "Your Grace?"

"Yes, my dear?"

"I am curious about something, and I thought perhaps you could help me."

"I shall if I can."

"I have heard a story. I don't know the people involved, of

course. But I wondered what you should do in such a case."

He patted her hand and smiled. "Tell me the case, my dear. And I shall tell you what I would do."

"Well . . ." Now that she had begun, she wasn't so sure this was a good idea.

"Go on."

"Well, Dezzie was telling me about a young woman who loves an artist—a sculptor, I believe. But her mother won't give them permission to marry. The young woman is—is of the ton, you see."

He nodded. "Then of course her mother won't give permission. A woman doesn't marry beneath her."

Hardly daring to look at him, she examined her gloves. "Why not?"

"It just isn't done."

The same old argument. "You said that. But it hardly seems fair."

He frowned. "The world is not noted for its fairness."

She pulled at her glove. "This man is a good person—a fine, honorable person."

"Then he should tell this young woman good-bye."

Licia raised her head. "But why? He loves her and she loves him. They could be happy together."

"Be sensible, Licia. An artist, you say. He's young and unknown, isn't he?"

She was forced to agree. "Yes. That is, I suppose, so."

His frown deepened. "Then he will not have the proper means to support her."

Men! They used the poorest excuses.

"But what if she doesn't care for the frivolities of fashionable life? What if she wants only to live a quiet life with the man she loves?"

His frown had become a scowl. "You seem to have an intense interest in this young woman. Is she someone you know?"

"Oh, no." She hastened to reassure him. "I just don't think it's fair. If two people love each other, they should be together." For some unaccountable reason she wanted to cry. "But I forget, Your Grace, that you don't hold with love. So you would find all this foolishness."

His scowl grew even fiercer. "That was unworthy of you, Miss Dudley. I tell you the same things any peer would tell you."

"Quite so!" She was all out of sorts with him. Still, she wanted to help Penelope. She managed a conciliating smile. "I don't suppose you can easily imagine yourself in such a sad case—in love and all. But exert yourself a little. Try to imagine what you should do."

He ran a hand across his brow. "As you suggest, I find it most difficult to imagine myself in such a case. But if I were . . . is this woman very young?"

"No. She's . . . I believe Dezzie said she's older. More nearly our age."

"I see." He examined his cuffs. "Then I should do the manly thing. Approach her mama and state my case."

"And if her mama refused you?"

"I . . . I suppose I might ask some person of consequence to intercede, to vouch for me—providing I could find one."

Her breath caught in her throat. But no, he would not do that. He was clearly against such unions. She swallowed over the lump in her throat. "And if that was unsuccessful?"

"I . . . Miss Dudley, your questions are most difficult to answer."

"You told Mama you would run off with me."

"Yes, but that was a special case."

141

"I see. And now you are saying that it is not the thing to do."

"Well, I . . ."

She was entirely distraught. "I knew it," she began. "You have no feeling, no—"

He took her gloved hands in his. "Miss Dudley, Licia. You are unfair to me. These unknown people, are they more important to you than my friendship?"

"No, of course not." Nothing was more important to her than he. When he looked at her like that, when he held her hands . . . She pulled her fingers loose. "But I am concerned about fairness. The principle of the thing, you see."

He raised an eyebrow. "The principle, is it? Well, my dear, I'm afraid the world isn't much for principle, either. I don't think this young woman has much chance for happiness. A man so far beneath—"

"Licia!" She turned to find an accusing Dezzie, her mouth rounding into an outraged *0*.

"I told Ravenworth about the young woman who loves a sculptor." Urgently Licia pressed Dezzie's arm. Please, let her understand. "I was taken with what you told me the other day. So I asked his grace what he would do in a like case."

Comprehension dawned in Dezzie's eyes, and slowly Licia let out her breath.

"Yes, it is a dreadfully sad case. I am so in love myself that I sympathize with all such people." Dezzie's eyes sparkled. "And did the duke have a solution?"

Ravenworth shook his head. "Not really. Such cases are difficult."

Dezzie frowned. "Well, I should think a man of your parts could do *something*. Go to Parliament and make a law." And Dezzie stalked off.

Ravenworth turned. "Your sister . . ."

"I know." Licia sighed. "She grows more like Mama every day."

The duke frowned. "Poor Lockwood."

Worried as she was about Penelope, Licia had to smile. "Don't fret, Your Grace. Dezzie loves Lockwood. He'll be able to control her, as Papa controlled Mama."

"I suppose so."

Licia wanted to get back to the subject at hand. "So if a direct attack on the mama failed, you would enlist the help of someone powerful. And if that failed and Gretna Green was your only recourse—"

His scowl grew fiercer. "You must . . . you must know that Gretna Green is no solution. A young woman of breeding should not be subjected to such an indignity."

"But if she loves—"

"If he loves her, he will find some other way."

She stared at him. "But you just said there is no other way."

This was not working as she had hoped. Penelope was right. She could look for no help from the duke.

"Come," he said, giving her a smile that looked patently false. "Let us get some lemonade."

It took Licia several days to feel once more in good accord with his grace. Not that she denied the veracity of his statements. She herself would have said the same things before she knew about Penelope, before she had met Harry Bates. Before, she admitted to herself, she knew what it was to love someone she couldn't have. Though in her case the reasons were different; still, she felt she knew something of Penelope's pain.

Toward the end of the week Ravenworth sent word that he would take them Friday next to see Kean. Licia tried to feel excited about it. Everyone was talking about Kean's feeling for Nature, about the marvelously natural effects he brought to his roles.

But Licia was laboring under a heavy load of worry. As August approached, Penelope's elopement grew more imminent. And more frightening. Licia was sure Aunt Hortense would disown her daughter. Mama might not, considering that she, herself, had run off with Papa.

But even if she didn't, Penelope would be lost to her cousin. As Harry's wife she would not have funds for visits to the country. And Licia, once she had prevailed upon Mama to return to the peace and quiet of York, never wanted to come to London again.

And that brought her 'round to Ravenworth. Possibly, if she stayed in town she could have him for a friend. But she knew, somehow, that that would be even more painful than not seeing him at all.

She found that she could not really imagine what it would be like not to see him. He had become so much a part of her life. The old days of contentment seemed bland and uninteresting. But they were the best she could hope for now.

And so the night of the theater party arrived. Penelope, whose expression had been growing more melancholy daily, tried to put on a cheerful face. But Licia could see the strain beneath the smile. "Oh, my dear," she said as they descended the great stairs. "I wish there were some way I could help."

Penelope only shook her head.

Ravenworth smiled as he handed them into the carriage— Dezzie and Penelope and Licia. "Your mama and Aunt Hortense will follow in the other carriage," he said, sending Licia a smile.

She tried to return it, to behave in a normal fashion. "I am eager to see Mr. Kean."

Dezzie sighed. "Will the viscount be there?"

"I believe so," Ravenworth replied. "His mama has commanded his company."

"His mama?"

"Yes."

Dezzie withdrew into silence.

"And your mama," Ravenworth said to Licia, "how is she?"

"Well," said Licia. "Quite well."

Penelope chuckled, the first time Licia had heard her do so in some time. "Aunt Dorothea is quite taken. She speaks of nothing but the Duke of Wellington, and in the most glowing terms."

Dezzie smiled. "She plans to invite him to my wedding. And yours, of course."

"Of course," repeated his grace in that dry tone he sometimes affected.

Licia swallowed a sigh. "Dezzie. Wellington is a very busy man. He may not have time."

Dezzie's laugh was lighthearted. "Oh, Licia. I know that! You mustn't think me such a goose. Now, Your Grace, what is the play for tonight?"

The duke sent her an amused smile. "I believe it is *The Merchant of Venice*."

Dezzie frowned. "Oh, dear. I was hoping it would be *Hamlet*."

His grace chuckled. "Come now, Dezzie. The path of true love has been made smooth for you. What need have you of Ophelia's laments?"

"None at all," replied Dezzie with a bright smile.

But once they had reached the duke's box, her smile turned sour. First, Mama decided that this time Dezzie must sit in the front. And then Dezzie spied Lockwood.

"There he is!" she cried excitedly and was just about to wave when the duke leaned forward and touched her arm.

"I should not do that," he whispered. "Lockwood's mama is a dragon for proper decorum."

Dezzie subsided immediately, whispering, "Yes, Your Grace. Thank you, Your Grace."

Licia swallowed a little smile. When it came to Lockwood, Dezzie would do anything.

But as the duke leaned back Licia saw he was still frowning. "What is it, Your Grace?"

"Nothing," he began. Then, seeing her disbelieving expression, he leaned closer to whisper into her ear, "My sister has been balking. She wanted someone higher for him, a nobleman's daughter."

"Oh." A cold hand closed 'round her heart. "She will not . . ." She could not finish the sentence.

Ravenworth covered her gloved hand with his. "My dear, do not take on so. It will be all right. Mama and I will bring her 'round."

"I hope so." Their continued whispering had brought their heads quite close together. For a moment dizziness threatened to engulf her. She wanted so desperately to lean her head upon his shoulder, to feel his arm around her. She struggled with these thoughts and with her worry for Dezzie. But, she told herself, she need have no fear for Dezzie. If Ravenworth said he would make it right, he would.

When the play began, Licia found it difficult to concentrate. She was familiar with the story, of course, but she had not seen the actual play before.

"Why, that's not Shylock," Mama observed plaintively. "He hasn't any red wig."

"Kean doesn't use a wig," the duke explained. "He does not believe the role is comic."

"Not comic?" cried Mama. "Why, everyone—"

"Dorothea, please!" Aunt Hortense used her most quelling look. "I should like to *hear* the play."

Mama lapsed into silence, but the set of her shoulders told Licia plainly that she had not changed her mind about a thing.

"Well," she said when intermission came, "that was the strangest thing. Why should he play Shylock in that peculiar fashion?"

"Because," replied Penelope with a bitterness that caused Licia's heart to beat faster, "because Shylock is a human being, a person with feelings."

Mama looked puzzled. "I don't see how that can be. He's a moneylender, a—"

"Aunt Dorothea!" Penelope's eyes were growing dangerously bright. "Weren't you listening? That's the whole point. That it doesn't matter who we are. Rich or poor, Christian or Jew. We are all *people*. We all suffer the same pains."

Mama digested this for some moments. Then she sighed. "These things are too difficult for me. I don't know why people are always changing things. Why can't they leave things the way they were? I have always laughed at Shylock. And now I cannot. It is most distressing."

The duke and Licia exchanged glances. "I am—" she began.

"Oh, no!"

Dezzie's wail made the duke turn toward her in alarm. "What is it?"

"There are ladies there, in the box with Lockwood. And he is . . . he is talking to them! Oh, this is—"

"Dezzie." The duke's tone was low but commanding. "Compose yourself immediately. Smile a little. Say something to your aunt."

"But—"

The duke was insistent. "The eyes of the ton are upon you. And Lockwood's mama is watching. You must act the lady. Believe me, this is of vital importance."

A sigh came from Dezzie, but she nodded and smiled at Mama. Still, from behind her, Licia heard the muttered words. "I hate him. Oh, I hate him! How could he do this to me?"

❋ *14* ❋

The next afternoon found Dezzie still in a fulminating mood. The three young women were gathered in Penelope's rooms. Licia, seated on a lyre-backed chair, watched with some misgivings while her sister paced in indignation and Penelope endeavored to calm her.

"Lockwood must listen to his mama," Penelope pointed out. "You know she controls the purse strings."

"That is no excuse!" Dezzie stopped her pacing to stamp in exasperation. "Look at the awful manner in which he behaved! Laughing and chatting with those horrible creatures. And not coming near me the entire evening!" She stamped her foot again. "It is inexcusable."

Licia sighed. She had problems enough without having to listen to Dezzie carry on. But if Dezzie lost Lockwood, everything they had gone through would be wasted. Licia couldn't stand that. "Dezzie, calm down. You know the viscount loves you." And how fortunate she was to know such a thing. "He was just trying to please his mama."

"I hate her, too," Dezzie cried, "the mean old dragon. She wants to keep him away from me."

Since Ravenworth had told her essentially the same thing, Licia could not give her sister much comfort.

But fortunately Penelope intervened. "Dezzie, you are being quite pea-brained. You know Licia is right. You know Lockwood loves you. You must just be patient. It will work out."

Licia, seeing Penelope's pain-filled eyes, wanted to shake

some sense into her sister. What right had Dezzie to build a little imaginary nothing into a tremendous obstacle to her happiness when poor Penelope had to face very real, very difficult obstacles? And Licia herself was in even worse case. At least Penelope knew she was loved. Licia didn't even have that bittersweet comfort.

"It will all work out," Penelope repeated in a soothing tone. "Now, why don't you go talk to your mama about wedding plans?"

Dezzie shook her head, her golden curls bouncing vehemently. "I am never going to marry such an insensitive, uncaring—"

"Then," said Penelope, her voice sharp enough to make Dezzie's eyes widen in astonishment, "go tell your mama that! But for pity's sake, spare us any more of these ridiculous diatribes!"

"Well, I never!" And Dezzie flounced out, an unconscious imitation of Mama that, had Licia not felt so melancholy, would have set her to laughing. As it was, she merely sighed.

When the door had closed behind Dezzie with rather more force than was necessary, Penelope turned with a contrite smile. "I'm sorry, Cousin. But I simply could not take another complaint. The way is so smooth for them."

Licia nodded. "I know. Dezzie can be quite a trial." She frowned. "But you know Ravenworth told me Lockwood's mama is against his marrying Dezzie."

"And *she* doesn't even know her." Penelope threw herself down on the chaise. "Sorry, Cousin. But my nerves are all unstrung. And Dezzie is not much help." She frowned. "I wish we had run off before. Then all this terrible waiting would be over." She pressed a hand to her forehead. "I have such frightening dreams."

She sat up, clasping a pillow to her. "Oh, Licia, I don't

want to hurt Mama. You know I don't. But I cannot give Harry up. He is such a wonderful man."

"I know." In spite of all her efforts, tears rose in Licia's eyes.

Penelope sprang to her feet. "Oh, dear! I am being just as insensitive as Dezzie! Pouring all my woes on you when you've more than enough of your own."

"I shall be all right," Licia said, getting to her feet too. With great effort she managed a smile. "Come, let us go join the others. I am quite sure Dezzie has *not* told Mama that the wedding is off."

Later, as they all sat at their needlework in the drawing room, a carriage could be heard pulling up outside. Dezzie flew to the window. "It's him!" she cried. "Oh, I shall make him—"

A loud cough from Penelope reminded her that Mama was still ignorant of any disagreement with the viscount and should remain that way. "I shall make him welcome," Dezzie muttered, coming back to her chair.

Aunt Hortense shook her head. "Young women these days, they're so flighty."

"She's just in love," observed Mama, mangling another stitch. "Licia knows."

Licia looked up in surprise. She did know, most painfully. But she was too old to go running off to the window whenever a carriage arrived, much as her heart might prompt her to do so. No, she must sit quietly and hide her disappointment that the duke was not with his nephew.

"The Viscount Lockwood," announced the butler. "And the Duke of Ravenworth."

Licia's needle slipped, and she gave her finger a vicious stab. Trust Dezzie only to speak of the one *she* was waiting for. Licia put her finger to her mouth.

Lockwood went directly to Dezzie, who greeted him with a frosty smile that left him plainly bewildered.

Ravenworth came to Licia. "Good afternoon." He glanced at the finger she still held to her lips, and his eyes twinkled. "An injury?"

"I accidentally pricked myself. It is nothing." Her eyes were on Dezzie and the frosty reception she was according her suitor. "Suggest a walk in the garden or a carriage ride," she whispered urgently to the duke.

The duke raised an eyebrow, but he said to the others, "The weather is lovely. Shall we take a carriage ride?"

"I don't wish . . ." began Dezzie truculently.

"Then a walk in the garden. I insist." And Ravenworth had the young ladies on their feet and out the French doors before Dezzie could do more than glare at him.

In the courtyard Dezzie stood firm, gazing coldly at the man she claimed to love. "I'm not taking a single step with *him*."

"All right," said Ravenworth with a sigh. "Kindly tell me what is going on here. We come to make a simple call and you treat us like French spies."

"He," cried Dezzie, pointing a trembling finger at the viscount, "is worse than a spy! He betrayed me!"

Lockwood paled and pulled at his cravat. "Dezzie, my love, I didn't." He turned to his uncle. "Explain it to her, Ravenworth."

The duke shrugged. "I did that last night. You must learn to manage your own affairs."

"But . . ."

Ravenworth ignored him and offered Licia his arm. "Shall we walk a little?"

She was not eager to leave Dezzie while she was in such a

state. But something in the duke's eyes made her link her arm obediently through his and move away. Still, she tried to look back over her shoulder at the young people.

"Let them be," said Ravenworth. "They must deal with this themselves."

She did not understand this attitude on his part. "But surely you could put it straight."

He smiled. "I am flattered at your regard for my diplomatic capacities," he said. "But in this case they won't serve. First off, it's unwise for the two of them to depend on me to settle their squabbles. After all, I shall not always be available. And second, it is not reasons that Dezzie really wants. I gave her those last night. It is reassurance of Lockwood's feelings for her that she actually seeks. And she can have that only from him."

Licia stared at him in fascination. "How did you come to know so much about love when you do not hold with it?"

Ravenworth frowned. "It is not love with which I quarrel but the institution of marriage."

Licia felt her heart fluttering. Perhaps all along he had loved that other woman; perhaps she was someone unsuitable for marriage. Did that mean Licia could enlist his aid for Penelope?

"But the institution of marriage has recently undergone a marked change in my perceptions," he continued.

Her heart jumped so suddenly that her step faltered and she had to clutch at his arm. That woman, the one he'd bought the painting for. He meant to marry her. "It has?" she managed to get out.

"Yes. I have come to see that a marriage based on love may be feasible, after all."

"I see." She got the words out. She even managed to add "It is very kind of you to delay your plans till Dezzie is wed.

Your lady must be—" suddenly her voice failed her.

"She is a fine lady. And she will wait for me," he said, his voice confident. But his eyes held the strangest uneasy look. She could not believe that any sensible woman would refuse him. Yet he appeared to fear just that.

She felt quite confused. Ravenworth was obviously a man who could sway Aunt Hortense's mind on the matter of Harry Bates. But if they asked him and he refused . . . she would have to leave the matter up to Penelope.

It was quite some time before she and Penelope had any time alone. After many protestations of love on his part and frosty looks on hers, Lockwood and Dezzie had made up. And the five of them had all gone for a carriage ride, after all.

Then, upon their return, Dezzie went off to discuss wedding plans with Mama, and Licia and Penelope were at last alone.

Licia followed her cousin into her room. "Penelope, we must talk."

Penelope closed the door. "Of course, Cousin. What is it?"

"I think we should ask Ravenworth to help you."

"No!" Penelope paled. "He would think it all foolishness. You know how he is about love. And he would tell Mama."

"Perhaps not. He said some things this afternoon—"

"You didn't tell him?"

"Of course not."

In her agitation Penelope crossed and recrossed the room. "Then what happened?"

"We discussed your case, a hypothetical case. And he said the man should get some powerful person to intercede on his behalf."

Penelope frowned. "David said that?"

"Yes."

"And he said the man should go to the mama and declare himself."

Penelope twisted her hands. "Harry wants to do that. But I told him no. Mama might send me away. I tell you, Licia, if I am denied Harry, my life will have no meaning."

"Penelope!" Licia remembered Penelope's words about the bridge. She might not have meant them, but still . . .

"I do not mean to alarm you," her cousin said. "But that is how it is. Without Harry my life is quite empty." She smiled. "But do not fear. It will not come to that. Harry will take me to Gretna Green."

"But Raven—"

"No." Penelope eyed her cousin sternly. "I know David. He will not help me in this. Licia, you must give me your solemn promise. Not a word to David. Not under any circumstances."

"But—"

"Give me your word."

There was no hope for it. She could see Penelope would not be swayed. "All right, I promise. I will not tell Ravenworth anything. No matter what."

"Good," said Penelope, obviously relieved. "I am much afraid that if he knew, David would ruin everything."

It was not Ravenworth who threatened to bring everyone's plans to ruination, however, but Mama herself. Though in this case she did it quite unwittingly.

They were sitting in the drawing room one warm afternoon a week or so later, stitching away at their needlepoint, when Dezzie hurried to the window. "I thought I heard a carriage," she exclaimed. "It's them."

Licia's heart contracted. It was ridiculous, of course, to feel so pleased just at the prospect of seeing him, but she could not help it.

"Oh, my," murmured Dezzie.

Alerted by her tone, Licia looked up. "What is it?"

"Something's wrong. Lockwood looks terrible. And the duke—"

"Dezzie, really." Aunt Hortense gave her a discouraging look. "It's not the thing for ladies to go peeking between the curtains at their visitors. Do come and sit down. You will learn soon enough why they are here."

Dezzie crossed the room and obediently resumed her seat. She even picked up her needlepoint, but Licia saw that her hands were trembling. Something had certainly frightened her.

And then the butler announced the visitors. One look at Ravenworth's black scowl was enough to inform her what had set Dezzie to trembling. And Lockwood looked so pale, she half expected him to collapse there on the floor.

The sight of the duke in such a mood made it difficult for Licia to speak. But Penelope was not similarly affected. "David, for pity's sake, do not scowl so! It makes you look uncommonly ferocious."

To Licia's surprise his grace ignored them both. He crossed the room to stand before Mama. "Mrs. Dudley," he began in a voice that made Licia shiver.

Mama, pulling at a recalcitrant stitch, did not look up. "Now, Your Grace, I do wish you would learn to call me 'Mama'."

"Madame!"

The duke's words thundered through the drawing room and brought a whimper from Dezzie. Mama merely looked up.

156

"Why," the duke demanded, "do you wish to bring ruin and unhappiness upon your own children?"

Mama's mouth rounded into an *0* of astonishment. "I, Your Grace? Why, what a thing to say! I want my girls to be happy."

"Then why have you destroyed my nephew's chance of winning your daughter?"

Dezzie's eyes went to Lockwood. "Oh no! What did she do?"

"She sent a message to the *Times*," the embarrassed young man related, pulling at his cravat as though it would strangle him.

Dezzie looked bewildered. "A message?"

Ravenworth swung to face her. "Yes. The announcement of your betrothal to Lockwood." His eyes went briefly to Licia. "And that of Licia to me."

Licia bit her lip in vexation. No wonder he was so irate. They had never meant to let it get this far. He must really be put out. And the woman he'd been uneasy about . . . this must have upset her.

"I'm sure I don't know what all the fuss is about," Mama said complacently. "You've both been courting for weeks. So I just sent a piece to the paper."

"Oh, Mama," Dezzie wailed.

"It is customary," said Ravenworth in chilling tones, "to consult the parties in question."

Mama shrugged. "It didn't seem necessary."

"And so in your usual empty-headed fashion—"

"See here, Your Grace," Aunt Hortense said, interrupting. "There's no need to fly up in the boughs. True, Dorothea might have—"

"She has almost certainly ruined Dezzie's chances with my nephew."

Dezzie burst into tears and Lockwood hurried to comfort her.

Aunt Hortense raised an eyebrow. "Now, Ravenworth, you needn't make it into a Cheltenham tragedy."

"It has the makings of a real tragedy, I fear. Amanda wanted Lockwood to wed higher. Have you forgotten what a stickler she is for propriety? And now Mrs. Dudley has gone and put a piece in the paper before Amanda's consent has been properly given."

Aunt Hortense frowned. "Oh, dear. I'm afraid you're right."

"My sister was almost ready to give her consent"—the duke fixed a stern eye on Mama—"until you bungled things."

To Licia's absolute surprise Mama covered her face with her hands and burst into tears. "Oh, dear," she said, sobbing. "I . . . am . . . sorry."

Ravenworth stood like one stunned. And Licia was in no better case. She could not remember ever having heard Mama say she was sorry.

The duke sent Licia a pleading look. Evidently a sobbing woman was an unfamiliar sight to him. Rousing herself, she hurried to Mama's side and put a comforting arm around her. "There, there, Mama." She looked up at the duke. "Please, isn't there something we can do?"

Ravenworth's scowl had faded to bewilderment. "I—I shall see what I can do. Mama and I are calling on Amanda later this afternoon." He paused. "Perhaps you should go with us."

"Your Grace!" How could he *dream* of taking Mama into such a situation?

"Yes," he said, nodding. "You must go with us. You and Licia. And Lady Chester, if you will."

"Of course I will," agreed Aunt Hortense. "But really, do you think it wise to—"

"I do," said the duke. He turned, glaring at Mama. "And you must not speak unless spoken to."

Mama nodded.

"And you must not, under any circumstances, mention Dr. Graham's celebrated bed."

Mama sniffed. "Very well. But I can't see why you take on so. It was quite a famous bed and . . . oh, all right. I shall not mention it."

The duke made a small bow. "Very good. Now I suggest you get dressed for visiting. We'll be back in an hour."

The door had barely closed behind him before Mama turned to Licia. "He's just like your papa," she said. "You're going to be very happy."

Trooping up the stairs with the others, Licia could only wish that it would be so.

Amanda, Lady Lockwood was a tiny woman with a face dominated by the hawkish Ravenworth nose and eyes that seemed to drill into one's soul. No wonder, Licia thought, that her son stood in awe of her.

They sat in the Viscountess's drawing room—Lockwood with his mama on one side and a subdued Dezzie on the other. To Lady Lockwood's right sat her mama, the dowager duchess, and to her right the duke. Mama, with Licia on one side and Aunt Hortense on the other, completed the circle.

Mama seemed completely cowed, and Licia prayed that they might get through this visit in properly decorous fashion. But knowing Mama, she was doubtful.

Ravenworth's sister fixed her gimlet eyes on Mama. "I understand," she said in a voice that would cut glass, "that you did not think my son good enough for your daughter." Here she cast such a look on Dezzie that the poor thing quite began to tremble.

Mama looked to Ravenworth, and, seeing his nod, tried a weak smile. "That is true, Your Ladyship. But that was before I knew the young man. And before I knew that His Grace—"

The duke cleared his throat, and Mama lapsed into silence.

"I believe you are from the country." This remark Lady Lockwood addressed to Licia. And she pronounced the word *country* as though it left a bad taste in her mouth.

"From York, Your Ladyship," Licia replied, wondering how this cold creature could be kin to the kind dowager duchess and to his grace.

She risked a look at Ravenworth, but his expression revealed nothing. His eyes were fixed on Mama, almost as though by looking at her he could keep her from saying the wrong thing. And perhaps he could. Licia devoutly hoped so.

"Dear Amanda," the dowager duchess told her daughter, "Mrs. Dudley is sorry to have caused you any discomfort with her announcement. She was just carried away with happiness for her girls. Licia is to wed Ravenworth, you know."

With his sister's eyes on her Licia fought hard to keep her composure. No one must suspect that it was all a sham.

"Mrs. Dudley did not think to consult me, either," the dowager went on. "And I admit to feeling a little miffed. But I do want my children to be happy. My grandchildren too."

Lady Lockwood gave this the barest of nods. "So," she said, turning to Licia, "you are to wed Ravenworth."

"Yes, Your Ladyship." She could feel his worried eyes on her. She must bear up under this.

"Well"—Lady Lockwood actually smiled—"you are to be

congratulated. No one thought he would go off. How did you bring it about?"

The blood flooded Licia's cheeks. "I—I do not know."

Lady Lockwood's eyes gleamed. "Nonsense. Every general knows how he won the battle."

"I know," said Mama.

Every eye in the room focused on her. Lady Lockwood leaned forward. "Do tell me."

"I cannot." Mama glanced triumphantly at the duke. "I am forbidden to speak."

The duke's sister frowned. "Forbidden? What nonsense. Come, tell me at once."

Mama shook her head. "I cannot. The duke has forbidden it."

Licia and Ravenworth exchanged glances. His slight shrug told her he had no idea what was going on in Mama's mind.

His sister turned to him. "Tell her she may speak," she said. "I am dying to know."

The duke looked bewildered. "First tell me, do you give Lockwood your consent?"

"Yes, yes. They may marry."

Dezzie half squealed, and Lockwood took her hand in his.

His mother paid them little mind. "Now, let her tell me," she repeated to her brother.

The duke shrugged. "Very well, she may tell you." He looked to Licia. "Whatever she thinks she knows."

Mama smiled. "I do know. It was Dr. Graham's celebrated bed."

Ravenworth groaned, but his sister and Mama both ignored him.

"Dr. Graham's bed!" Lady Lockwood exclaimed. "You know about it? Oh, marvelous! Absolutely marvelous. My Lockwood used to tell me such stories of that bed. Come,

161

let's go into the library. You must tell me everything you know."

And while the others sat, mouths agape, Lady Lockwood led Mama away.

The dowager duchess was the first to recover. She burst into delighted laughter. "Hortense, I cannot believe it. All these years I thought Amanda was as prim as they come. There's hope for her yet."

Licia turned to the duke. "I am sorry," she said. "I had no idea what Mama meant."

His grace managed a rueful smile. "Of course you didn't."

Licia sighed. "How could she believe that the place of my . . . that the bed could gain me your love?"

He shook his head. "Your mama's mind works in a most peculiar fashion." His hand covered hers, giving her a strange sensation in the pit of her stomach and causing her breath to catch in her throat in a most uncomfortable fashion. "But," he continued, "we should rejoice. After all, we have gained our objective."

❊ 15 ❊

On Friday next, Ravenworth and Lockwood arrived to escort them all to the theater. Dezzie glowed as Lockwood helped her into the first carriage. "One month," he said. "In one month you'll be mine."

Dezzie giggled. Ravenworth, having just helped the older ladies into the second carriage, raised an eyebrow. "The two of you sound like you're fresh from the nursery. All this billing and cooing."

Lockwood coughed. "No need to be so cold, old chap. You'll put Miss Dudley off with such talk."

Ravenworth smiled, but there was something different about his eyes, something Licia couldn't understand. "Miss Dudley knows my sentiments on marriage," he said.

Penelope chuckled. "Come, David. No pontificating on the institution's limitations if you please. Let the young people be happy."

Ravenworth grimaced. "You wound me, Pen." He glanced at Licia. "Besides, has no one told you that my sentiments have changed? I am now one of the institution's staunchest supporters."

"That he is!" cried Lockwood. "Why, just the other— ouch! I say, Ravenworth, watch those long legs of yours. That hurt!"

Licia bit her bottom lip. The duke was not a clumsy man. The kick he had just delivered to his nephew had not been an accident, but, she suspected, an attempt to shut Lockwood up. What had the viscount been about to divulge?

163

But she was not to find out. Lockwood turned to Dezzie. "Tonight you'll get to see Kean do Hamlet." His face grew properly melancholy. " 'To be or not to be,' " he intoned dramatically.

Dezzie gazed at him with adoring eyes, but Ravenworth raised a hand. "Please, do let us wait for the play."

Lockwood grinned and turned his attentions to Dezzie.

Licia, stealing a look at Penelope, swallowed a sigh. She was worried by the brightness of her cousin's eyes, the fevered flush of her cheeks. Setting the date for Dezzie's wedding had also meant setting the date for Penelope's elopement. As soon as Dezzie was safely married, Penelope meant to be on her way to Gretna Green with Harry Bates. All need for pretense would be over then. But Penelope's elopement would mean the end of Licia's friendship with the duke. He would undoubtedly be angry at her complicity in such a thing.

"Whoever would have thought it," Penelope said, "your sister and Dezzie's mama becoming bosom bows. And over that ridiculous bed!"

Ravenworth shook his head. "I have never understood Amanda. She is not like me. She is not like Mama. If I did not know better, I should say she does not belong in our family. But after all, she has our father's nose. And who can go against evidence like that?"

Licia smiled at this attempt to amuse. She must exert herself, she thought, to make this evening enjoyable. There would not be very many more. "Well, at least the bed served a useful purpose." She cast Ravenworth a glance. "I have grown used to hearing the tale. In fact, I may begin to relate it myself—with sufficient elaborations, of course."

Ravenworth's eyes gleamed with humor. "It would make you the talk of the ton. But, alas, you would not do it."

"I should hope not!" cried Lockwood, pulling at his cravat. "My mama may be dealing famously with Dezzie's at the moment. But what she talks about in private and what she—"

"Miss Dudley is bamming us," the duke interjected with a smile. "Has love so addled your wits that you cannot tell?"

Lockwood grinned. "Yes, I believe it has. But I like it."

"And you, David," said Penelope. "Has love affected your wits too?"

Licia's heart threatened to stop right then and there. How could Penelope talk to him like that, and when she knew this was all a sham?

"Perhaps it has," he replied. "Tell me, what do you think?"

Penelope shook her head. "Oh, no, you don't," she said. "I am not hazarding a guess on that."

Ravenworth turned to Licia. "Then I shall ask you, my dear, do my wits appear addled?"

In the light of the carriage lamps his expression was whimsical. Her heart rose up in her throat, but she endeavored to carry this thing off. "No, Your Grace. I'm afraid your wits are as sound as ever."

Dezzie laughed. "Well, I'm afraid Mama's are not. She is constantly mooning over the great Wellington."

Penelope smiled brightly. Too brightly, Licia thought. "It is all this romance going on around her," Penelope observed. "Aunt Dorothea has been affected by it. First it was Kemble. Now it is Wellington."

"And soon it will be someone else," Licia told her sister. "Do not trouble yourself about it."

Lockwood frowned. "It is a shade difficult, though. Can't she pick on a chap who hasn't a wife? My mama—"

Ravenworth clapped him on the shoulder. "Don't go off

having a worry fit now, my boy. You're young and in love. Enjoy it."

Lockwood's face cleared. "You're quite right," he said, and turned back to Dezzie.

The street outside Drury Lane was thronged with carriages. Chattering and nodding, glittering nobility packed the walk and made its way into the theater.

"Keep together now," Ravenworth told the young women as he helped them descend from the barouche. "Lockwood, you stay with them till I get the others."

As soon as the duke was gone, Licia leaned toward Penelope. "Are you feeling quite well?" she asked softly.

"I am fine," her cousin replied. "I am counting the days till Dezzie's wedding." Her eyes grew brighter. "I am quite looking forward to it."

"Penelope, please . . ."

Penelope frowned. "I have waited long enough," she whispered. "I must do this thing. And I must do it soon."

"Penelope! You haven't . . . you didn't let . . ."

Penelope laughed, that harsh sound so unlike her usual soft laughter. "No, Licia, I haven't. I would have. But he is an honorable man."

"Penelope!"

"Do not look so shocked, Cousin. I am safe. Quiet now. Here comes David with your mama and mine."

Amid considerable confusion Ravenworth got them all inside to his box and properly seated. Then he turned to Licia. "You're looking pale, my dear. Are you feeling quite the thing?"

His solicitous look and the tenderness in his eyes caused a great lump to rise in her throat. She swallowed hastily. "I . . . I am fine," she lied. "Just . . ."

"David?" said Mama. Licia winced. In spite of his refusal to call her Mama, Mama had begun to call the duke by his Christian name.

He gave Licia's hand a comforting pat. "Yes, Mrs. Dudley?"

"I wish you to warn me ahead of time. This Kean fellow quite ruined my enjoyment of *The Merchant of Venice*." She cast Penelope a dark look. "Shylock, a person like us! Indeed!"

She turned back to the duke. "So tonight I do not wish to be surprised. What is this Kean person going to do to poor Hamlet?"

The duke smiled. "I'm afraid to tell you, ma'am, but he will probably make him more human too."

"Oh, yes, ma'am," Lockwood said eagerly. "Kean's a great actor. Top of the trees."

Mama sniffed. "I do not see how anyone could improve on Mr. Kemble's presentation of the melancholy Dane. It was divine. Though the man himself was quite unfriendly, actually a boor."

Ravenworth exchanged glances with Licia, and she smiled. He was really quite kind with Mama. Considering all he had gone through since that first day and the story of the bed, he had been more than kind.

She was about to tell him so, but the play began. It was the most amazing thing. The man who had given such humanity to Shylock now made Hamlet into a person one could understand. There was no dramatic posturing, no heroic poses or thundering soliloquies. Nothing but a man—a young, sorrowful man—caught in the throes of indecision, pulled to and fro by his warring emotions.

When the curtain closed for intermission, Ravenworth turned to Licia. "Well, what is your opinion?"

Before she could answer, Mama turned 'round in her seat. "You are quite right, Your Grace. This man is marvelous. Why, for the first time I actually understand Hamlet. He's just a poor, unhappy boy who doesn't know what to do." She swung 'round again. "Hortense, did you see . . ."

"And you?" the duke asked Licia. "What did you think?"

"He's wonderful. So different from Kemble."

"And he must be much friendlier," said Mama swinging 'round again. "When the play is over, we must go to the Green Room to meet him."

Foreseeing another scene like that with Kemble, Licia was about to protest, but his grace spoke first. "That will be fine, Mrs. Dudley."

"And I shall be sure to compliment him," Mama continued, giving the duke a smile. "Such a great man."

After the play was over they proceeded to the Green Room. There the great man held court in the usual fashion. To Licia he looked distinctly uncomfortable, as though he wished to be somewhere else. Anywhere else. But perhaps that was only her own wish plaguing her.

"You *will* introduce me," Mama began, hanging on Ravenworth's arm.

"The other ladies . . ." he said.

"Go ahead," said Aunt Hortense. "I've no desire to meet the man."

"Nor I," said Penelope.

Licia considered begging off. But not to know what Mama was saying was probably worse than hearing it.

Up close, the great man looked weary. His eyes were bloodshot and there was about him a hint of imminent disaster.

And then he smiled and Licia forgot everything.

"Ravenworth!" he said. "How good to see you. And this is the one who caught you. What a lucky fellow you are."

"Thank you," said his grace. "I think so too."

Licia flushed. She could not get accustomed to these compliments.

Mama tugged impatiently at the duke's arm. "Your Grace . . ."

"And this," said the duke, "is her mother, Mrs. Dudley."

"Oh, Mr. Kean, what a marvelous talent you have," Mama gushed. "Why, I was telling David, here, that for the first time I really understand poor Hamlet. Tell me, please, why you behaved as you did when you saw the ghost." And Mama led the actor off as if no one else in the room existed.

Ravenworth chuckled. "Your mama never ceases to amaze me," he said. "She is one of a kind."

Licia nodded. She only wished that that kind were a little easier to deal with.

Some time later the crowd in the Green Room had begun to thin out and Aunt Hortense said, "I really think we should be going home. Now where is Dorothea?"

Licia, who had been happily discussing the play with the duke, was suddenly reminded that she had not seen Mama since she'd gone off with the actor.

"I shall look for her," Ravenworth volunteered. "You wait here."

"Nonsense," said Aunt Hortense. "Two searchers are better than one." And off she went too.

Licia scanned the room.

"That won't help," said Penelope with a frown. "She went out some moments ago."

"Out?"

Penelope nodded. "I thought it strange at the time, but

then I got busy talking and forgot. Oh, Licia! She asked me where the dressing rooms are! You don't suppose she's gone there?"

"Oh, no. Mama knows better than—"

"Then where else could she have gone?"

"Oh, dear, I had better go look. Do keep the others here. I'll be back soon."

The narrow hall was dark. Licia hurried along it, stopping now and then to peer at the names on the doors.

There it was at last—Edmund Kean. She knocked softly but there was no answer. She pushed the door open.

"Oh, Mr. Ke—" Mama's eyes widened in astonishment. "Licia! What are you doing here?"

"Mama!" Hastily Licia stepped in and pulled the door shut behind her. "What are *you* doing here?"

"I am waiting for Mr. Kean, of course."

"Mama! Mr. Kean is a married man!"

Mama sniffed. "He's an actor." She put on an air of innocence. "Besides, I am here to discuss *Hamlet*. Nothing else." And she patted her hair in a gesture that gave the lie to her words.

"Mama, do think! The scandal. Lockwood's mama. And the duke's. You will ruin our wedding plans!"

"Don't be ridiculous."

"Mama! You are here—alone in the man's dressing room. You must leave immediately—before anyone finds you here."

Mama considered this.

"Remember," Licia continued, "you came to London for Dezzie's come-out, to find her a proper husband. You don't want to ruin her life."

"That's true," Mama agreed. "Well, perhaps you are right." She got to her feet. "But it's all a lot of silly botheration."

"Yes, Mama. But please hurry. Mama! What *are* you looking for?"

"My new kid gloves. I'm quite sure I had them when I came in. Now where have I put them?"

"Mama, you must leave at once. I shall find them. Do go. And do not tell a soul where you have been."

Mama went, still muttering. And Licia began a systematic search of the room. It would be a miracle, she thought, searching through the clutter of playbooks and costumes, if they managed to get Dezzie safely to her wedding.

At last the gloves turned up, stuffed half under a cushion on the threadbare settee. Licia snatched them up and hurried toward the door.

And just as she reached it, it opened. "Well, well," said Kean, his eyes growing brighter. "What have we here?"

"I was lo—"

Ravenworth appeared in the doorway, his face registering shock at the sight of her. "Licia, whatever are you doing here?"

"I—I—shall tell you later," she stammered, easing past him. "Good evening, Mr. Kean."

Ravenworth followed her down the hall. "Licia! Miss Dudley!" His hand on her arm stopped her.

"Yes, Your Grace?"

"I think an explanation is in order."

"Why?"

It was a stupid thing to say, and his expression told her so.

"I find you alone in an actor's dressing room and you ask me why I think you should explain?"

"We are not really . . . that is, I mean nothing to you."

His face grew grim. "Miss Dudley, may I remind you that we have an agreement? I thought you wanted to see Dezzie safely married. If this should get back to my sister—"

"That is why I didn't tell you in front of Kean." Her hands were trembling and she hid them in the folds of her skirt. "I went there to find Mama."

"I did not see—"

"I sent her out. So she shouldn't be found there."

"And why didn't you go too?"

"Because she had lost her gloves. I was trying to find them."

"And did you?"

"Yes." She held them out. "Here they are."

He let out a big sigh and offered her his arm. "Whatever possessed her to do such a thing?"

"With Mama it is hard to say."

The others were waiting near the door of the Green Room. Licia heard the duke's quick intake of breath and felt the arm under her hand stiffen. And then she saw! Mama was wearing gloves.

"Licia, where have you been?" Mama's tone was plaintive. "It's quite impolite of you to keep us waiting. We are all weary and ready to go home."

"But, Mama, you knew where I was."

Mama put on her best look of innocence. "Why, Licia, I'm sure I haven't the foggiest notion. I've been all the time here in the Green Room, except for just a moment when I stepped into the hall."

"Mama—"

"Enough," said the duke. "Your mother is right. It is time to leave."

The ride home was made in silence. Dezzie and Lockwood were lost in each other's eyes. Penelope gazed into nothingness, no doubt thinking of Harry. But Licia had little thought for any of them. All her attention was on Ravenworth, whose face, in the light of the carriage lamps, was grimmer than she had ever seen it.

Finally, unable to bear it any longer, she turned to him. "Your Grace, I should—"

"Do not bother," he said in a voice so cold that Penelope shifted her gaze to him.

"But I want to—" Licia began.

"And I do not." The words were quiet, courteous, and even, but the look in his eyes was not. Licia subsided into a miserable silence. He suspected her. He actually suspected her of lying to him. In truth, he suspected her of something far worse.

🌸 *16* 🌸

The next week passed, a miserable week in which Dezzie's wedding grew ever nearer and Ravenworth sent word that he was called out of town on land-reform business. Licia, remembering the coldness of his eyes when he had last left her, doubted the truth of that excuse. Perhaps it was all a story, so he need never see her again.

She was tormenting herself in this fashion one afternoon when Penelope appeared at her chamber door. "Come in," said Licia, "sit down. You look dreadfully pale."

"It's just a few more days," Penelope said, her lips trembling.

Licia nodded. "Aren't you frightened?"

Penelope sank down on the bed. "Of running away? Yes. Of marrying Harry? Not at all. I would go anywhere to be with Harry." She sighed. "I am most frightened by the fear that something will go wrong." She glanced at the door. "We are making our final plans. And I must ask you to make a visit to the gallery."

"But why? Why don't you go?"

"We decided it would be safer not to see each other until it's time to leave. That way people will not remember seeing us together." She stared hard at Licia. "We need those first few hours. Please, you must do all you can to delay Ravenworth."

Licia pulled nervously at her sash. This was not an easy task her cousin had set for her. "I will do what I can. You know I will."

"That's all I ask. Now, will you take this note to Harry?"

Licia nodded. The role of secret messenger was not at all her to liking, but Penelope needed her help. "Give me the note. I only hope I don't see anyone I know."

Several hours later she pushed open the door of Turner's gallery and gazed nervously around. There were very few people about. Perhaps it would be easier than she had thought. She opened her reticule and extracted the note. If she could just pass it to Harry and go home, she would be forever grateful.

The door to the inner room opened. "Mr. Bates," she began, hurrying toward him. "I have—"

Something in his expression made her hesitate, stop. And then she saw why. Ravenworth stepped out the door behind him.

"I—I have come to see the newest painting," she said, stammering. "And to take a last look at *Frosty Morning*, if it is still here."

Ravenworth's expression did not falter. "You have sold *Frosty Morning*, then?"

"Yes, Your Grace." Harry looked nervous. He was not good at lying. "But the buyer has left it here temporarily."

"Good. Then we may look at it again."

"Yes. Yes, of course." Harry was plainly flustered, and Licia herself hardly knew how to behave. She had thought Ravenworth safely off in the country. To find him here was definitely unsettling.

She must give the note to Harry, but his grace did not seem to be leaving. His demeanor was not as cold as it had been when he left her after the play, but she still felt uncomfortable with him.

However, she took the arm he offered her and they followed Harry to the farthest corner of the gallery. There he set out the painting.

"Oh." The word slipped from Licia's lips as for a moment she forgot everything except the beauty before her. "It is so very real," she said finally. "I almost believe I could reach out and touch the frost."

"And it would sting your fingertips before it melted there," Ravenworth said.

"Yes," she agreed. "That's it perfectly."

They stood for some moments, admiring the painting. But Licia was brought quickly back to reality. The folded note seemed to be burning its way through her palm.

Harry raised his head. "If you will excuse me, Your Grace, I see some others have come in. I must take care of them. Please, take your time and look all you please."

"Thank you," said the duke in absentminded tones. His whole attention seemed centered on the painting.

"Yes," said Licia, extending the hand that hid the note. "Thank you very much."

Harry's hand met hers, and when they parted, he had the note. He was gone immediately, nervously sticking a hand in his pocket as he went. Licia allowed herself a small sigh of relief.

"Miss Dudley," said the duke.

Licia looked up at him. "Yes, Your Grace?"

"I know it is not my place. You have told me that we are nothing to each other. But still, you must have a care."

Panic filled her. She'd been so careful. He couldn't have seen! She squared her shoulders. "I don't know what you mean. I am most careful."

"Not of your reputation. Fortunately Kean is a friend of mine."

Her panic eased. He had not seen then.

"He will not tell anyone of your little escapade," the duke continued.

The last week had seen her nerves wound tighter and tighter. Now they snapped. "It was not an escapade," she retorted sharply. "And I was not lying to you. It all happened exactly as I said."

He frowned. "It couldn't have. When we rejoined the others, your mama was wearing her gloves."

"Yes, because she had stuffed them in her reticule and forgotten them."

"But the gloves you were carrying . . ."

"Obviously belonged to someone else. I returned them to Mr. Kean the next morning. By messenger."

"But that night your mother claimed—"

The last thread of her patience broke. "Your Grace, I find this questioning most irritating. You've no right! And . . . and if you must know, I told Mama not to breathe a word about where she'd been. And for once she listened to me."

"But there's—"

"I don't care to discuss anything else," Licia said. "I thank you for your part in arranging Dezzie's happiness. And now, good day!"

"Wa—"

But Licia swept on, out the door, and into the carriage. "Home," she told the driver. "Take me home."

Later, sitting with the others in the drawing room, she wondered if she had been too hasty. Perhaps she should have stayed longer, listened to what he had to say. But he had no right ordering her about. Now, if he loved her as Harry Bates loved Penelope, then he might have been within his rights to question her so closely.

She glanced up. Across the room, Penelope sat beside her

mama, placidly stitching on a chair cover that she might very likely never finish. Her expression was serene, but Licia recognized the small signs of strain—a slight tightening round her mouth, a certain stiffness to the set of her head.

As Mama continued to prattle on about Dezzie's wedding, Penelope's tension increased. And no wonder—she and Harry should have been planning a wedding too.

Dezzie, overflowing with nervous energy, flitted from one window to the next, pausing at each to peer out.

"Dezzie, my dear," Aunt Hortense remonstrated. "Do sit down. It's quite distracting to have you continually on the go."

"I'm sorry, Aunt, truly I am. But I am so excited. When I think about it, I want to laugh and cry at the same time."

Aunt Hortense chuckled. "My, it is wonderful to be young and in love."

Penelope, her face gone white, stabbed her finger and winced.

"Yes," said Licia quickly. "It is quite wonderful."

"Oh, why doesn't he come?" Dezzie cried.

"You are expecting Lockwood?" her aunt asked.

"Yes, he sent word that he is coming. And he asked us all to be here. He's bringing a surprise."

"A present?" asked Mama, her eyes lighting up.

Dezzie frowned. "I'm not really sure. The note said only that it was a surprise."

"Did he mention that the duke has returned?" Licia asked.

"No. It was quite a short note. Oh, I do wonder what the surprise is."

Aunt Hortense smiled. "You'll know soon enough, child. Just be patient."

Dezzie hurried to the window again. "He's here! And"—she glanced at Licia—"his grace is with him. And—"

"Dezzie, sit down." Aunt Hortense's tone was grave. "I've

spoken to you about this before. You must learn to comport yourself with dignity."

"Yes, Aunt." Dezzie sank into a chair, her eyes on the doorway. But she was on her feet again the moment Herberts announced Lockwood. "Lockwood," she cried, rushing to his side.

"Dezzie, my dear." The viscount looked nervous. He was already pulling at his cravat.

Licia's heart sank. Surely Lady Lockwood had not changed her mind.

"The Duke of Ravenworth, the dowager duchess, and guest," intoned Herberts.

Across the room, Penelope turned deathly white. Ravenworth and his mother stood in the doorway. And behind them, his face drawn with anxiety, stood Harry Bates.

"Come in," said Aunt Hortense. "Well, Mr. Yates—no, Bates—is there something wrong with my painting?"

Harry looked startled. "No, milady."

"This is not about a painting," said the dowager. "This is about something far more personal."

Penelope gave a little moan, and Licia hurried to her side.

"Well, then," said Aunt Hortense, "don't just stand there. Get on with it."

The dowager exchanged a look with her son and settled into a chair. The duke motioned for Harry to come forward.

Harry looked hagged, and Penelope, supported by Licia's arm, was in no better case. Harry stopped in front of Penelope's mother. "I have come to you, as a gentleman should, to ask for your daughter's hand in marriage."

For a moment Aunt Hortense appeared not to have heard him. Then she laughed. "Really, Ravenworth, this joke is in poor taste."

"It is not a joke," said Mama calmly. "The young man is in earnest."

Aunt Hortense bristled. "This is outrageous! How dare you?"

Harry drew himself up to his full height. "I dare because I love her."

"You cannot—"

"And I love him," said Penelope, shaking off Licia's arm and hurrying to stand by the man she loved.

"Ungrateful child," sputtered Aunt Hortense.

"That is exactly what my mama said to me," Mama observed. "And I could never understand why. I did not fall in love to spite her."

Aunt Hortense looked about to explode, her face turning a dangerous shade of crimson.

"You should be grateful," said the dowager to her. "They were planning to run off."

"Penelope!"

"I love him, Mama. And he loves me. We don't ask for much. Only your blessing."

"You shall never—"

"Wait," said his grace, his tone commanding. "I advised Mr. Bates to come here. To declare himself."

At that moment Licia loved him more than she ever could have supposed possible.

"But why?" Aunt Hortense demanded. "And how did you get involved in this?"

"It came to my attention"—he cast Licia a dark look—"that Penelope was planning to run off. Mr. Bates had wanted to come to you before."

"But I was afraid," Penelope said simply.

"So," continued Ravenworth, "after I heard the whole story I was convinced of Mr. Bates's good character."

Aunt Hortense grimaced. "A painter. It's inconceiv—"

"It's love," said his grace, and his mama nodded gravely. "Now," he went on, "as I see it, you have two options. You can forbid the marriage. In which case you will lose your daughter and my friendship."

"And mine," added the dowager duchess.

Penelope gave Ravenworth a look of complete gratitude. "Thank you," she said.

He nodded and continued to address her mama. "Or you can accept the inevitable. Take Mr. Bates as son-in-law. Keep your loving daughter and eventually you will have grandchildren to dangle on your knee."

"I am sorry to have deceived you, Mama," Penelope said bravely. "But I am not sorry to love Harry. I shall always love him."

"The ton," said Aunt Hortense. "Think of the scandal."

"What is most important," inquired the duke, "what people say of you or your daughter's happiness?"

"But a painter!"

"Hortense," said Mama. "Do not refine so on what the man *does*. Look at *him*. You can see that he loves her."

And indeed, the two standing there, their hands entwined, seemed to be lit with a quiet glow.

Aunt Hortense heaved a great sigh. "Very well, you have my blessing. But nothing more."

"I should accept nothing more," said Harry firmly.

"Excellent," said Mama as she resumed her stitching. "Now all three of you shall be wed."

And that was when the enormity of it hit Licia. Tears welled up in her eyes, and while the others were busy with congratulations, she slipped out through the French doors. Their charade was over. The others would wed, and she would go back to York. Probably without even a chance to—

"You will not escape me that easily."

She turned to find Ravenworth close behind her. "Your Grace, I . . ." She wiped hastily at her eyes.

"Crying tears of joy?" he inquired.

"I . . . I am happy for Penelope."

"Of course you are."

"And you must be pleased that now there is no more need for subterfuge."

"Oh, yes, very happy."

"Then we are agreed. We can safely tell the others the truth."

"If we can ascertain it."

She stared at him. Her heart was breaking and he was talking in riddles. "I do not understand."

"Nor did I," he said gravely, "not for some time. But we shall puzzle it out. Come, let us sit here on the bench."

She let him lead her there, and she settled herself. "There is nothing to puzzle," she said, fighting the tears. "It is all very clear."

He settled beside her. "Perhaps to you. But humor me in this. Answer for me a few questions." He raised a hand. "I know . . . I have no right to ask them. But perhaps you will tell me, anyway. The first day I discovered you giving the note to Mr. Bates it was not about the paintings but about a personal matter. For Penelope. Is that right?"

"Yes."

"And earlier today when you passed Mr. Bates the note—"

"You saw?"

He smiled. "I fear you are not the sort to conduct clandestine affairs. Your face gives you away. As soon as you departed, I confronted Mr. Bates." He smiled ruefully. "Rather forcefully, I'm afraid."

"Poor Mr. Bates."

"You still do not understand." He sighed. "Well, let us go on. When you told me the story about the sculptor—it was Pen and Mr. Bates you were talking about?"

"Of course."

"You did not consider that I might think it was about you?"

"Of course not." This was all very painful to her. "Please, Your Grace, could we not get to the point? I'm sure the lady who's been waiting for you will be glad to hear that her waiting is over."

He raised an eyebrow. "I am not sure she will have me."

"Not sure? But that is impossible. Any woman—" She stopped, uncomfortably aware of what she'd been saying.

"Any woman would what?" he inquired, leaning closer.

She could not meet his eyes. "Would be pleased to be your wife."

"Would *you?*"

The shock of it made her tremble. It was too cruel. "Really, Your Grace, I am not a suitable—"

"But if you were," he went on, his voice relentless. He would not even leave her her pride.

"If I were," she cried, "then I should say yes, I would marry you."

"Thank God!" he cried, sweeping her into his arms and covering her lips with his. Her senses all seemed to go crazy, and when he released her mouth, she could only lie against his waistcoat and whisper, "I do not understand. The agreement is over. There is no need . . ."

"There is every need," his grace said softly. "I love you, Licia. I love you and want to marry you."

Her head was swimming. "But the woman, the one you bought *Frosty Morning* for . . ."

"You," he said tenderly. "It has always been you. Since

the first day I saw you and your mama started in on the story of the celebrated bed."

"But you did not say . . ."

He kissed the tip of her nose. "I did not know your feelings. I hoped through our agreement that you would come to love me." He frowned. "I did not expect to be consumed with jealousy, however. Seeing you pass notes to a man put me into a jealous rage. And finding you in Kean's dressing room . . ."

He sighed and drew her closer. "I am sorry about that, my love. But I was so afraid of losing you."

She burrowed closer against him. "That will never happen," she said. "My, it was good of you to help Penelope. I wanted her to come to you, but she was afraid."

"She was right to be," he admitted. "At any other time I would not have helped her. I know, my love." He put a detaining finger on her lips. "She deserved help. But it was loving you that made me give it."

He kissed her forehead. "When I thought about losing you, I knew how Pen must feel. And I had to help her." He grinned. "I confess, too, that I thought it might help establish me in your good graces."

She breathed a small sigh of contentment. "Oh, David, I cannot quite believe it. We are really going to get married."

"Yes, indeed," he said, drawing her closer still. "But I must insist on one thing: Your mama must not mention that horrible bed again."

Licia laughed. "Oh, my dear, you know we cannot prevent it. Why, she will want to tell it to our child!"

"There is no need to blush," he said, pulling her to her feet. "I hope we shall have many children." And he took her in his arms.